The Maltese Holiday

Also By
Nicole Mullaney

Ivy & Mistletoe
Deck the Heart
Magic in Mount Holly (coming in 2021)

Also check out works by Ethan Dulane

Joy & Hope

For Adult Romance check out works by Nikki A Lamers

The Unforgettable Series:
The Unforgettable Summer
Unforgettable Nights
Unforgettable Dreams
Unforgettable Memories
The Unforgettable One
Unforgettable Mistakes (coming in 2021)

The Home Duet:
Dreams Lost and Found
Finding Home

The Maltese Holiday

By Nicole A Mullaney

Based on the Screenplay by Candy Cain

Table of Contents

Copyright

Frey Dreams, an imprint of Nikki A Lamers

ISBN 978-1-951185-07-7 (Paperback)
ISBN 978-1-951185-08-4 (E-book)

Cover Design by Heartly Creations

Image by Benjamin Bryant

Dedication

To Michael and Craig,
our partners in this crazy journey called "life".

Chapter 1

Shea

The jingle of bells followed by a deep baritone voice, brings me out of a deep sleep. I blink a few times, adjusting to the light and stretch my arms above my head, attempting to wake up. I glance towards my window and realize the sunlight is just starting to come through the crack in my blinds. What time is it? I reach for my phone and turn off my alarm, glancing at the time. A slow smile spreads across my face at the reminder on my screen. Today is the day I'm leaving for Malta with my best friend for the holidays. I'm so excited!

I open my camera on my phone and tap video. I glance at the screen, my own brown eyes looking back at me and make sure my long brown hair isn't sticking up or anything before I press record. I grin wide and start talking, "Good morning everyone! Shea here and as you can see I literally just woke up." I giggle, feeling giddy about the trip and continue, "You're about to come on the biggest 'Sheacation' ever! It's 7:35am here in New York and today is the big day. Me and my best friend, Kristen, are about to spend the holidays in Malta!" My smile grows as I continue, "Kristen and I have been best friends since college and this is our last big trip before she gets married," I announce, gleefully. "We have some amazing stuff planned and I am bringing you with me every step of the way. So, make sure to like, follow, subscribe and keep up to date with all of my updates. Ciao!" I declare and end my vlog.

I sit up in my queen-sized bed with a natural wood headboard with short square posts and a beautiful scroll carved in the middle, matching my dresser, armoire and nightstand. I reach out and pet my dog, sprawled out on my navy blue and white paisley patterned quilt right next to me. "Good morning, Toby!" Lifting his white and tan head, his ears perk up as he looks at me, his tail beginning to wag as he wakes up. I climb out of bed and encourage him, "Come on, let's go!" He jumps down from the bed and follows me out of my bedroom. I let him outside and grab us both some breakfast.

I reach for my phone and tap Kristen's name, wanting to make sure she's awake and getting ready to leave for the airport. Her voicemail picks up and I leave a message, "Good morning sleepy-head! Wake up and call me because we are going to Malta!" I reiterate cheerfully. "Alright, call me back. Bye," I mumble and tap to end the call.

After breakfast I brush my teeth before trying to call Kristen again, surprised she hasn't called me back yet. Her voicemail picks up again and I sigh in disappointment. "Hey! I haven't heard from you yet, just want to make sure you're up and ready to go. Call me back. Bye." Hopefully she's just too busy getting ready and isn't looking at her phone.

I make my way back to my room and pack a few more last minute things into my suitcase. Then I make my way over to my armoire, to pull out my clothes for today, before trying Kristen again. Her voicemail picks up and I grimace, attempting to keep my frustration at bay. I'll see her soon when we leave for the airport if nothing else. "Hey. It's been a little while. Just want to make sure the car is coming and everything is on time. Give me a call back. Bye!" I disconnect the call and set my phone down on my dresser.

I scoop up my clothes for today and go back to my bathroom to get myself ready. I jump in the shower and get dressed. Since we're traveling today, I want to be comfortable. So, I'm wearing dark blue Capri jeans, a soft, and pale pink sweater with matching pink and white sneakers. I dry my long, wavy brown hair and pull it back into a loose French braid to keep it out of my face; also knowing it will be comfortable against the seat of the plane. I'm relatively petite at five feet, four inches. Days like today, when I'm about to get on a plane for a long flight, I'm thankful I'll have more legroom.

I walk back out to my bedroom and pick up my cell phone. Noticing no missed calls or messages, I attempt to call Kristen again, but her voicemail picks up again. I take a deep breath, reminding myself she wouldn't miss this. We've been planning this trip forever. It's going to be fine. I exhale slowly and announce, "Kristen! I haven't heard from you yet. Ah, I just want to make sure everything is okay. Um, I'm so excited! Call me back. Bye!"

I grab Toby's leash, knowing the dog sitter should be here any minute to pick him up. I walk down the stairs, with him scampering behind me, just as the doorbell rings. I head straight for the door and lean down, giving my dog some love and attention. He wags his tail and pants with his tongue hanging out of his mouth as I say goodbye. "I'll see you soon. Be good and Merry Christmas! I love you," I croon and give him a kiss on the top of his soft head. I stand up and hand the leash over to the dog sitter with a broad smile, "Thank you and Merry Christmas!"

"Merry Christmas!" he replies as he takes the leash from me. "Have a good trip. Toby is in good hands," he adds.

"Thank you," I repeat. I wave and shut the door behind him.

I grab my suitcases and pull them up to the door, finally ready to go. I glance out the window and peek at

10

my phone, checking the time. "The car should be here by now," I mumble to myself, starting to become anxious. I don't even know what company Kristen booked the car with and she's not answering her phone. I take a deep breath to calm my nerves, as I wait for a few more minutes. I glance out the window again, before I pull up the phone number for a cab company and tap the number. I breathe a sigh of relief as the woman confirms, "A driver will be there in five minutes to pick you up."

"Thank you," I reply gratefully. I end the call and tap Kristen's name one more time before I head out the door. "Hey, so I haven't heard from you," I begin, "hope everything is okay. Don't really know what's going on. The car never showed, but it's all good!" I declare, attempting to remain positive. "I called a cab and I'll see you at the airport!" I proclaim. "Yay, Malta!" I add.

I hang up the phone, just as the cab pulls up. I roll my luggage out to the car and the driver steps out, helping me load my suitcases into the trunk. "Thank you," I tell him and slip into the back seat, the black leather cool to my touch.

I remain quiet throughout most of the drive to the airport, my stomach churning with anxiety. I bite my lower lip, staring out the window at the snow-covered streets and wondering why Kristen hasn't called me back. That's not like her. I hope she's okay. I grab my phone, calling her again. "Kristen, I'm really worried!" I declare, my voice full of concern. "I'm in the car and almost at the airport. I'll check in and go right to the gate. We're really cutting it close!" I emphasize. "Where are you?" I softly prompt, pleading.

Might as well do another vlog to keep my mind occupied until we get there. I switch over to video and hold my phone out in front of me before I press record. "Hey there! This video was supposed to be me and

Kristen in the back of a limo, drinking mimosas on our way to the airport, but as you can see, it's a little different than expected." I slowly move my phone over, revealing the empty seat next to me, before returning to myself, my expression a little sad. "Kristen never showed and she hasn't answered her phone, but maybe she forgot to charge it last night or something?" I say as more of a question, trying not to let my mind run wild. There has to be a good reason. She has to be okay. "I'm sure she's just waiting for me at the airport," I conclude, laughing. "And now I'm the one that's going to be late."

I heave a sigh and continue, "The snow this morning caused some traffic, but the snow stopped and the flight is still on time. Don't worry!" I prod, grinning. "I'm sure I'm going to get there on time; at least with enough time to check my bag and get to the gate." I purse my lips, thinking about when we first started talking about doing a trip and now it's finally happening. "Kristen and I have been planning this trip for over a year and a half. There's no way she'll miss it. She's definitely coming!" I emphasize, trying to convince myself it's the truth. "Okay, alright," I mumble. Taking a deep breath I state, "Ciao for now," and end the video.

I slip my phone into my pocket as we pull up to the airport. I climb out and get my bags out of the trunk, setting them down and slamming it shut. I hang my cranberry winter coat through my oversized black purse and sling the strap over my shoulder. Then I grasp the handle of my black suitcase and stride towards the front door of the small section of the airport, rolling my suitcase behind me.

I'm so excited to be going on this trip with my best friend for the holidays. It's been crazy at work lately and I really need the break. Although, since I'm a Photographer, I guess I'll be working some while I'm away too.

Discovering a new place like Malta off the coast of Italy is the perfect trip for us. There is so much for us to see and do. Plus, the resort we're staying at looks absolutely incredible from everything I've seen on-line as well as in the brochures Kristen got for us. I want to pull them out and look through them again when I get on the plane.

My phone rings just as I reach the building. I pause briefly to pull it out of my back pocket. I glance at the screen and grin, relief flooding me as my best friend, Kristen lights up the screen. She has a few inches on me in height and she's almost the opposite of me in looks with her straight, shoulder length blonde hair, bright blue eyes, pale skin, rosy cheeks and a bright smile. "Hi! I just got here. I know I'm running late. I'll hurry," I quickly blurt out before she has a chance to scold me for being late. Luckily there are only a few gates at this section of the airport, so I don't have too far to go.

The sliding glass doors open for me and I walk into the large, open hallway leading to security and the gates. Bathrooms are found on both sides, along with a few offices down a short hallway to my left.

"Well, I have to tell you something," she begins, sounding anxious.

"What's wrong?" I prompt, shaking my head, even though she can't see me. "Forget it. I'm going to go through security and you can tell me on the plane."

"You can't. I'm not there," she grumbles.

"What?" I ask, shocked. My heart drops into my stomach, fearing the worst. She's never late for anything.

"Shea," she begins, "I'm okay, but I'm not coming," she relents, with a heavy sigh.

I feel both relief and frustration crash into me with her words, immediately halting my footsteps. "What do you mean you're not coming?" I demand. "Kristen, I spent more than half my savings for this trip!" I remind her.

"I know and I'm sorry," she apologizes, sounding regretful. "Barnaby and I got into a major fight and I can't leave," she concedes.

I flinch at her admission. Of course he's the reason she's not coming. "Fight about what?" I question and begin walking towards security again.

"About going halfway around the world with a single woman before we get married," she answers, honestly.

I clench my teeth and take a deep breath to calm myself down, before I reply. "A single woman?" I repeat. "Kristen, I'm your best friend!" I argue.

"I know!" she agrees. "I told him that! But he's my fiancé and we're getting married in a month," she reiterates, as if she's trying to remind herself of the fact. "I don't want to leave when he's so angry," she claims, softly.

I wince, hating that she feels like this. He shouldn't make her feel this way, but there's not really anything I can do about it, except be there for her. Instead, I attempt to remind her about what she would be missing. "We've had this trip planned since you got engaged," I say as if she doesn't know. I hesitate for only a moment before I inquire, "You couldn't have cancelled earlier, so I could have at least tried to get my money back from insurance?"

"Shea, I'll pay you back," she insists.

"It's not about that, Krissie," I proclaim. "It was supposed to be our special trip before you get married," I remind her. "A once in a lifetime trip," I reiterate, feeling defeated.

"We can always go on other trips, Shea. I can't always find another husband," she contends.

I stutter step and stop abruptly, shaking my head. "I can't believe you just said that," I grumble, both hurt and surprised.

"Come over and I'll give you a check. I'll pay you back for everything," she offers.

I grimace and shake my head in denial, even though she can't see me. "Don't be ridiculous. Where are you going to get that kind of money?" I probe.

"Barnaby said he would give it to you," she claims.

I huff a humorless laugh. "No way. He hates me," I state.

"He does not," she refutes, defending him like she always does. I wish she didn't feel like she had to do that, especially with me. She should always be able to talk to me about everything. I've never judged her for anything.

"He does," I insist. I heave a sigh and shake my head in realization. "He never was going to let you go on this trip, Krissie," I claim, irritably.

There's a crackle through the speakers built into the ceiling, alerting me to an upcoming announcement. "This is the last call for flight number 827 into Malta International Airport. At this time, all passengers are required to board."

Hearing the announcement, I make an instant decision. "I'm going," I proclaim, with a satisfied smile on my face.

"What?" she prompts, surprised.

"I'm still going on the trip," I repeat. "Have a Merry Christmas, Kristen," I state. "I'll see you when I get back." I continue walking towards security.

"Are you sure?" she questions.

"Yes," I firmly declare. "You might have a fiancé, but all I have is a once in a lifetime trip. I'm fine going by myself," I claim.

"But, you'll spend Christmas alone," she emphasizes.

"I would have spent it alone anyway. My family is going on the cruise, remember?" I remind her.

"Oh, right," she mumbles, sadly. "I'm sorry," she repeats.

I heave another sigh in defeat and concede, "I know you are." I stop in front of security and hand her my ticket and my ID. "I have to go, I'm at security," I inform her.

"Okay. Have a good flight," she stresses. "Let me know when you get there," she emphatically requests, her voice heavy with regret.

"I will. Bye," I say and tap the red button to end the call. I smile up at the security guard and immediately apologize. "Sorry."

She nods in acknowledgement, while glancing at me and then reviewing both my ID and ticket. "Have a nice flight," she tells me, pasting a smile on her face as she hands me back my things.

"Thank you," I reply. Then, I slip my ID inside my purse before swiftly making my way towards the gate, pulling my suitcase behind me.

I quickly stride through the airport, noticing the large holiday wreaths decorated with berries, pinecones, ribbons and bows on several of the walls. Colorful garland with colored lights adorn the front of the desks at each gate, with a small wreath or decoration hanging in the middle. I spot my gate with a large animated lit snowman sitting next to the desk, slowly putting the top hat on his head before taking it off and repeating the process over and over again.

I promptly make my way up to the desk keeping my focus on the desk clerk. He's about six feet tall and thin, with thick gray hair and a friendly smile. He's dressed similar to the other desk clerks with black dress pants, a white button down shirt, and displaying a small pin of the airline attached to his tie. Like the other desk clerks, his tie is his one distinguishing feature. His tie is

Christmas green with small red and white candy canes scattered all over it for the holidays. I'm determined not to miss my flight, now that I've decided I'm going without Kristen.

Chapter 2

Michael

I walk with my brother Daryl through the airport, about to board a plane with him on a trip that Beverly was supposed to be going on with him, not me. I keep glancing at him out of the corner of my eyes. He can't seem to stop fidgeting or questioning himself, if the look on his face is anything to go by. We look a lot alike, with a few minor differences. He's thirty-four, older than me by almost five years. We both have short, wavy, brown hair, but he has pale blue eyes like my mom, while I have emerald green eyes, like my dad. We both have a diamond shaped face with a strong jaw, but I have a small dimple on my chin, while he has one on his left cheek. We also have a similar lean build, but I'm five foot eleven, while he's six foot three.

We're both dressed comfortably for traveling, hoping to get some sleep on the flight. I need it and I'm positive Daryl does too, especially after having such a long day yesterday, or the whole week for that matter. I'm dressed in dark blue jeans and a long sleeve, olive green, crew neck sweatshirt and black sneakers. My brother is also in dark blue jeans, but with a gray half-zip pullover and gray sneakers. We both already checked our suitcases, but we each have a black backpack slung over a shoulder for our carry-on.

He scrunches his face up again, as he trudges slower and slower as we make it to the other side of security. I have to say something. "Will you chill out?" I request. "We're going to have a great time," I insist, hoping I'm able to help him feel better on this trip.

He winces at my comment, making me feel even worse. I can't blame him after what he's been through the past twenty-four hours. "This was supposed to be my honeymoon, Mike," he reiterates what we both already know.

"I know, but stop thinking about that," I plead. He huffs a humorless laugh and I continue, "You can't control what she did."

He sighs heavily and gives a slight shake of his head. He gulps and meets my gaze. "Beverly and I," he begins.

I immediately interrupt him, "Can you just not say her name, Daryl? She doesn't deserve you even mentioning her," I insist, irritably.

He cringes in response. He stops three steps short of the desk and shakes his head in exasperation. I turn around to look at him and he throws his hands up in the air in defeat. "I can't do this," he grumbles, shaking his head.

"Do what?" I prod.

"Instead of going on my honeymoon with my wife, I'm going on it with my brother," he states in response.

"Don't be ridiculous," I reply. Taking a step closer to him, I demand, "You're getting on that plane. We have to go," I claim.

He shakes his head and retorts, "No, we don't."

"Yeah, we do," I maintain. "I already took two weeks off to go on this trip with you," I remind him. "I can't get that time back."

He shrugs, like it's no big deal. "So you go," he suggests.

"What?" I question, with an arch of my eyebrows.

"Go without me," he replies. "You're a big boy," he adds, sarcastically. "You deserve a break anyway," he adds, softening his insult.

Daryl walks past me and closes the distance to the desk. I turn and reach for his arm, grasping it to stop him. "What do you mean?" I ask, for clarification.

"I'll go take care of mom. You've been with her since dad died. You need a break, little brother," he emphasizes. "You go have fun without me," he repeats.

"To Malta?" I balk.

"Yeah," he answers and nods his head for emphasis.

"I don't know anything about Malta," I argue.

He shrugs his shoulders and concurs, "Well, neither do I."

My eyes widen in surprise at his admission. "So why would you even go there?" I inquire, puzzled.

He grimaces and begins, "Cause Bev…"

I step towards him and immediately interrupt him, holding a finger up in warning. "Don't say her name!" I exclaim, hating what she's done to him.

"Fine!" he grumbles, in annoyance. "She who shall not be named chose it," he mutters, sarcastically.

I shake my head in disbelief. "And you just went along with it?" I prompt.

He runs his hand through his hair in frustration. "I told her she could pick where we would go for our honeymoon," he replies, bitterly.

"This is unbelievable," I mumble, continuing to shake my head.

"Mikey, go. Just go," he pleads. "Have a good time for me," he requests.

"I don't even know what language they speak," I claim. I suddenly feel slightly panicked at the thought of going to Malta without my brother. It's not that I can't go without him, but this was his trip, not mine. I was just going along to support him.

"They speak English," he informs me, rolling his eyes. "Here," he says. He reaches into his coat pocket and pulls out an envelope, immediately handing it over to me.

"What is this?" I prod, taking it from him.

"It's the full itinerary," he enlightens me, with a stiff smile. "I'll go change everything over into your name."

I stare at the envelope in shock as my brother turns around and approaches the desk. I force myself to move and reluctantly follow behind him, with a heavy sigh. "Hi," I hear him greet the desk agent.

"Daryl, wait!" I attempt to stop him one more time.

Daryl turns away from the desk and prompts, "What?"

"Come on, Man," I beg. "We get to spend Christmas together, just us. It's been a hard year," I plead, reminding him.

He visibly flinches at my comment. He sarcastically mumbles, "Tell me about it." My stomach twists, watching the expressions on his face go from pain, to anger, to disappointment, to regret and finally acceptance, without his sadness ever leaving his eyes. I hate that everything went wrong with Bev on top of everything else, but she's not good enough for him. I just want to help him. He stares at me for a moment before he relents and vocalizes more than he obviously wanted. "I just want to be with mom, okay?" he requests, begging me to understand.

"Angela is with mom," I remind him. "She doesn't need you," I reiterate.

"No, but I need her," he concedes. "You don't understand, Mikey," he complains. "Do you have any idea how humiliating it was for Beverly to leave me at the altar?" he flinches, as the question leaves his lips.

"I do," I insist, trying to let him know how much I hurt for him through my expression. "I was right next to you," I remind him. It felt like my own heart was breaking for my brother when I realized she wasn't coming. I always believed they weren't quite right for each other, but she's the one he wanted, so I supported him. Now, I want to be here for him again. That's the reason I'm standing here at the airport with him now, about to go on his honeymoon with him. I'd do anything for him, just like I know he'd do anything for me. He's my brother.

"I can't run away from this," he insists, seeming determined. "I need mom. I need to talk to her, or I'm going to go crazy," he claims.

"So call her," I suggest, hoping I can change his mind.

The desk clerk interrupts our conversation, "Gentlemen, I'm sorry to interrupt, but the door is about to close," he advises.

"Daryl, come on," I beg.

"Please, Mike. Will you please understand," he pleads.

I heave a sigh and drop my head in defeat. Then I look up at my brother, giving him a small smile in understanding. "Yeah. I do," I declare, sadly.

Daryl closes the distance between us and pulls me into a hug. He pats me on the back two times and I do the same, returning the gesture. "Thank you," Daryl murmurs, sincerely, as he takes a step back.

I nod my head in acknowledgement. "Okay. Let's go," I mumble. Then I turn towards the exit and take a step in that direction.

"No," Daryl refuses, reaching for me and stopping me this time. I face him and arch my eyebrows in question. He huffs a humorless laugh and continues, "I spent fifteen thousand dollars on this trip; one of us is getting on that plane. You go. Enjoy yourself," he insists.

He shrugs his shoulders and smirks as he adds, "Besides, maybe you'll meet someone."

A petite brunette runs up to the desk, appearing out of breath. "I'm so sorry! I'm here!" she broadcasts. I stare at her with wide eyes, the corners of my mouth twitching up in amusement at her entrance. "Oh. Sorry. I didn't mean to interrupt," she stammers, awkwardly, her face turning a deeper shade of red with each word. "I'll just wait my turn," she mumbles. She pastes a smile on her face and takes a giant step backward, exaggerating the movement.

"Alright," I murmur. I tear my eyes away from her and bring my focus back to my brother. "I'll go," I finally relent.

Daryl gives me a crooked smile, as if relieved by my response. "Try to have some fun, will you?" he prompts.

I give Daryl a small smile and nod my head in agreement. "Yeah, sure," I mumble, with a nod of my head. Stepping towards my brother I give him a hug with a firm pat on the back as he reciprocates the gesture.

I turn towards the gate agent and hold my ticket out. He scans my ticket and I turn and wave to Daryl as I walk through the door at the gate and down the short jet bridge to the plane. I step inside, the plane and look to my right, the first seats 11A-F. I grimace and look to my left, where a long navy blue curtain hangs from the ceiling all the way to the floor. A steward stands in front of the curtain, so I approach him and ask, "9C?"

He grins and reaches towards the curtain and pulls it back, holding it in place for me to walk through. "Right this way," he advises, politely.

"Thanks," I mumble. I step through the curtain, slightly relieved at the sight of the larger navy blue leather seats. At least I'll be more comfortable sleeping up here. I should've known these tickets were first class. Beverly probably insisted. I heave a sigh and find my seat on the right, next to the window, labeled 9C.

"Hot towel?" a stewardess offers. I look up and force a smile. She looks to be about the same age as my mom, with dark hair and brown eyes. She's grinning up at me and holding out a rolled hot towel between silver tongs.

I shake my head and remember my manners. "No, thanks," I mumble.

"Would you like something to drink besides water?" she questions.

I repeat, "No, thanks." Then I turn away and put my backpack under the seat in front of me and sit down in the soft and comfortable seat by the window. I buckle my seatbelt and lean back against the seat with a heavy sigh. I look out the window, watching the men and women in the reflective vests, loading and unloading suitcases, directing traffic or working on a plane.

I let my head fall back against the seat again and close my eyes. What am I doing? I shouldn't be going on Daryl's honeymoon by myself. This is ridiculous. How did I let him talk me into this? Maybe I should just get off the plane. Then again, it's not like I have anything to do. I don't have to work for the next two weeks and Daryl seemed to really want me to go. I know we can't get the money back and he wanted someone to enjoy it. But shouldn't I be home with my family? Especially now, it's Christmas. I grimace and attempt to straighten out my thoughts, completely confused as to what I should do. I don't know if this was really the right way to help him.

I hear a small squeal of excitement and I reflexively look for the source. My eyes crash into the same soft, sparkling, brown eyes I just saw at the gate. She's smiling brightly and talking to her phone, causing me to grimace. She stops at my row and glances at me. Oh, no. I cringe as realization dawns on me. Daryl gave her his seat. I sigh heavily and mutter under my breath, "Just great." She's the opposite of what I need right now. She's absolutely beautiful and obviously excited to be going to Malta. I don't think I can handle that much happiness at the moment.

Chapter 3

Shea

I rush up to the desk by the gate, not really registering anything yet. The gate agent looks up with a smile and prompts, "Ticket please?"

"Can I just use the restroom really quick?" I blurt out, not answering his question. "I promise I'll be really fast," I plead.

He hesitates before conceding, "Make it fast."

"Thank you!" I reply. I spin on my heel and run to the bathroom. I finish and wash my hands. I glance in the mirror, noticing how tired my big, brown eyes already look and this trip hasn't even started. I take a deep breath and grab my bags, as I make my way back out to the gate before the plane leaves without me.

After I'm done, I step into the hallway and pull my phone out, pressing record on the video. "Hey, guys!" I greet them. "So, I know she's not coming with me, but it's okay," I say, attempting to convince myself, "because I have you. I'm going to tell you guys all about my Malta trip and we're going to share the amazing experience together. So keep posted and watch my videos for more. Bye," I smile broadly and end the video, uploading it before slipping my phone back into my pocket.

I quickly make my way over to the desk and blurt out, "I'm so sorry! I'm here." Two good-looking guys in front of the desk stop their conversation and look at me, one smirking and the other scowling, not appearing too happy. I startle and take a step back. "Oh, I'm so sorry. I didn't mean to interrupt," I mumble awkwardly. "I'll just wait my turn," I add smiling wide. I take another step back and look around at nothing in particular, attempting to avoid their uncomfortable stares.

I watch as they appear to stop arguing and finish with the desk clerk. They step towards one another and hug briefly before one of the guys turns and walks through the door at the gate to board the plane. As I stand back, waiting, I can't help, but overhear the conversation between the taller man left at the desk, speaking with the gate agent. "Is it a problem that I'm not getting on the flight?" he inquires.

I grimace, his question reminding me of Kristen. "You're not the only one," I mumble under my breath.

"Did you check a bag?" the gate agent asks.

"Yes," he confirms.

"Let me help this lady out first," he pauses and gestures to me, "and then I'll see if there's an issue," the agent offers.

"Great, thanks," the man replies, with sigh of relief. Then he pulls his phone out as he steps off to the side and out of the way.

"Next," the gate agent calls.

I step up to the desk and hand him my ticket over the counter. "Here you go," I declare, smiling wide.

He scans my ticket and then frowns, causing my stomach to twist with sudden anxiety. "May I see some ID, please," he requests.

"Sure," I reply. I pull out my passport and hand it over to him. He flips it open and looks from my passport, to my ticket and then to the computer screen, his frown growing.

I gulp down the lump in my throat and question, "Is something wrong?"

He meets my gaze and gives me a sad smile. "Your ticket was assigned to a standby passenger when you didn't arrive for last call," he explains.

I gasp as my eyes widen in surprise. I knew I was late, but to give my seat away? "Can't you just give me another seat?" I solicit.

He shakes his head and replies regretfully, "No. The flight is completely booked," he reveals.

After everything, now I can't even go on the trip? The guy steps back towards the counter and interrupts, "Excuse me? I believe I can help," he offers.

"How?" I prompt.

"Here," he tells me, holding something out to me. My eyebrows draw down in confusion as I hesitantly reach for the paper he's holding. "Take my ticket," he proposes.

I look down at the paper, now in my hands and gasp in shock. "Excuse me?" I question, with wide eyes.

"Go ahead," he prods. "I don't want to go anymore," he claims.

"Are you serious?" I reiterate.

He heaves a sigh and nods his head in acknowledgement. "Yeah. It's a long story," he claims, offering me a sad smile.

"I don't think you can do that," I tell him. At the same time, my heart pounds hard against my ribcage, as I'm suddenly filled with hope. I look at the gate agent, needing clarification. "Can he do that?" I inquire.

He shrugs in response and informs us, "That's up to the two of you." I suppose it's kind of like me being on stand-by and having him offer me his seat instead.

I look up at him, attempting to tamp down my optimism, but I struggle to contain it. "Are you sure?" I ask. I hold my breath and bite my lip in nervous anticipation.

He nods his head firmly and declares, "Yes."

I grimace and inform him, "I can't afford another ticket."

He shakes his head and offers me a small smile. "I wasn't expecting any money. I can't get a refund anyway. Go ahead," he encourages. "Enjoy the trip."

I squeal in excitement and throw my arms around him, taking him by surprise and nearly knocking him over. He quickly regains his balance and awkwardly pats me on the back, returning the gesture. I step back, letting my arms fall to my sides as I grin broadly up at him. "Thank you so much!" I exclaim.

"You're welcome," he acknowledges. He gives me another small smile that doesn't reach his eyes. I wish I knew him well enough to say something to make him feel better. "Will you ask my brother to keep an eye out for my bags on the other side?" he requests. "In case I'm not able to get them off," he adds.

"Of course," I agree.

I spin on my heel, knowing I better hurry and get on the plane. I hand the gate agent the new ticket. He scans both my original ticket and the new one, swiftly tapping something into the computer. Then, he looks at me and grins politely. "Enjoy your flight," he proclaims.

"Thank you," I tell him. I look back at the kind stranger and reiterate, "Thank you! Merry Christmas!"

"Merry Christmas," he replies. He pastes a smile on his face and holds his hand up in a small wave.

I wave, just before I disappear through the door at the gate and pull out my phone as I make my way down the jet bridge. I hold my phone out in front of me and with a huge smile lighting up my face, I tap to record a video for my vlog. "Oh my gosh, guys!" I begin, with obvious excitement, rushing down the gangway. "You're not going to believe what just happened to me. I'm the last person to board the plane and I'm using someone else's ticket. Shout out to the handsome stranger who gave me his seat on my flight to Malta!" I praise. "Okay, keep following my story for all my updates over the next ten days. Bye!" I finish with a quick wave. I tap end and quickly add it to my story.

I step through the door of the plane and quickly find my way to my new seat, 9A. I grin even wider the moment I realize it's in first class, an upgrade from my seat in coach. I smile at the man, already sitting in the window seat. He heaves a sigh and runs his hand through his hair as if in irritation. I put my bag under the seat and I'm immediately offered a hot towel. I smile gratefully and take it from her. "Thank you," I acknowledge. I wipe my hands, enjoying the sudden warmth, before I return the towel to the tray.

"Would you like anything to drink?" she offers.

"Could I just have a water, please?" I request.

"Another one?" she clarifies, gesturing to the small bottle of water by my seat.

I feel my face heat with embarrassment and nod my head, requesting, "Please?"

She nods politely and acknowledges, "Of course."

I pull my phone out and tap the button to record another video. "Okay, guys, so the guy that gave me his seat, his ticket was for first class," I announce, grinning broadly, my mouth slightly open in shock. I'm so excited. This is going to be such an amazing flight! Okay, I'm thinking that I'm probably going to do so many updates to show you guys the food, the drinks, and all this kind of stuff," I prompt, exuberantly.

The guy sitting next to me narrows his eyes at me and interrupts, questioning, "Are you going to do be doing this the entire flight?"

My eyes widen and my eyebrows nearly hit my hairline in surprise. "Okay," I murmur awkwardly. "Um," I mumble, not quite sure what to say. "Bye," I whisper, with a small wave before I tap to end the video.

He rolls his eyes in annoyance and pulls a book out of his bag. He opens it and readjusts in his seat as he focuses on the book.

I drop my phone into my lap and look around me, taking everything in. As we turn down the runway and wait for final clearance, I attempt to look out the window. I want to look outside and watch the land disappear as we take off and increase our elevation. The guy next to me glares at me and I sit back, reluctantly watching from a little further away. We begin to pick up speed and I'm gently pushed back in my seat from the momentum. The nose of the plane tips up, as the wheels leave the ground. I watch as the ground slowly disappears and I finally settle back into my seat.

A little while later, the flight attendant comes around holding a notepad in one hand with a pen poised above it. "What can I bring you for dinner?" she inquires.

My eyes widen and I ask in surprise, "I get to choose?" She grins and points towards a laminated menu in the seat back in front of me. I quickly scan it and point to the lemon chicken with rice pilaf and mixed vegetables.

"And for him?" she questions, gesturing towards 9C.

I turn, looking at him and realize he's sleeping, or at least pretending to. I gently poke him in the side. He reaches up and lifts his mask, peeking out at me. The moment he meets my gaze, he glares at me, not giving me a chance to speak. Then, he covers his eyes with his mask again and turns his back to me. I grimace and glance up at the flight attendant and shrug. "Sorry," I apologize for him.

She gives me a grateful smile. "It's okay. I'll have something in case he's hungry later," she informs me. I nod in understanding as she moves on to the next row.

I'm looking through the airline's magazine, dreaming about different places I'd like to travel to, when she returns with my meal. I smile appreciatively as she sets a lemon chicken down in front of me. I'm impressed by how good it looks and smells. I grab my phone and tap in my code to unlock the screen. I have to tape this. I press record and point the camera at the food. "Did you know that the food in first class looks this good?" I pause and take a bite of the chicken, before I tap record again. "Mm, it tastes delicious too," I mumble. I wave and end the video to eat.

I attempt to ignore the guy next to me, who still has his back to me. That can't be very comfortable. I take another bite and he suddenly wakes. He stretches and unbuckles his seatbelt. Then he stands and climbs over me, bumping into my tray and not saying a word. I glare at his retreating back as he makes his way to the bathroom. I try to eat quickly, hoping I'm done before he returns. I finish my meal and move onto the apple pie. I moan in appreciation at the crisp, sweet taste. I'm quickly bumped out of my world, when he comes back and climbs over me to return to his seat causing me to grimace, but I bite my tongue, remaining silent.

Later, after all our food and drinks have been cleared and I've looked through the brochures again, I'm not sure what to do with myself. I look around to find most people are sleeping and only a few seem to be reading or watching a movie, but I can't seem to sit still. I'm so excited to be traveling, even though I am alone. I glance at the guy next to me, with a black mask over his eyes, finally looking relaxed. I have to admit, he doesn't seem quite so miserable while he's sleeping. I force my eyes away from him and pull out my phone. I tap record, attempting to keep my voice at a whisper and still be heard. "Alright, guys, we've been on the plane for about two and a half hours and everybody is sleeping, except for me," I begin.

"Or trying to," the man's deep voice grumbles next to me, sending unexpected chills down my spine.

My hand flies up to my mouth, covering it, as I try to hold back my amusement. "Sorry," I quietly apologize. He doesn't pull off his mask to acknowledge me. He doesn't even move. I roll my eyes and smirk, mouthing to my phone, "Whatever." Then I tap to end the video. I grimace and put my phone away before I sit back in my seat. I sigh and grab my mask. I slip it over my head and over my eyes as I close them, attempting to fall asleep. It takes me a while, but I do eventually drift off to sleep for a few hours.

Chapter 4

Shea

I hear the soft whirring sound of the airplane as I feel myself starting to wake up. My eyes momentarily remain closed, but a slow smile spreads across my face, the constant sound a subtle reminder that I'm really on vacation. I've been saving, waiting, and anticipating going to Malta for so long, I just want a moment to enjoy the feeling of it actually beginning before I'm fully awake. I do wish Kristen were here with me, but even without my best friend by my side, I'm determined to have a memorable trip.

I start becoming aware of my surroundings, even before I open my eyes. The whole right side of my body feels incredibly warm and cozy. I take a deep breath and exhale slowly, the faint scent of a musky cologne lingering in the air and causing my heart to pick up its pace. I move just a fraction and a soft gasp slips through my lips, as realization suddenly hits me like a truck. I'm leaning on my incredibly handsome, but also immensely grumpy neighbor's shoulder. My entire body automatically stiffens and heats in embarrassment as my heart pounds so hard, it feels like it might burst out of my chest. I slowly blink my eyes open, but all I see is the back of my silky, green, ivy and mistletoe sleep mask. I cautiously reach up and tug it off, squinting at the sudden brightness of the cabin. I stretch my hand down and tap the lever on the side of my seat, slowly raising the back of it. I can't help but wonder if the guy next to me is awake, but I'm afraid to even dare a glance in his direction after using him for a pillow for probably most of the night.

Barely moments later, I hear and feel him moving around. I discreetly peek over at him, just as he slips off his own simple, black sleep mask. I really hope I didn't wake him. I can't believe I fell asleep on him. It's like something you see in the movies, but I fell asleep on a jerk, the complete opposite of prince charming. Then again, if he was already awake and didn't react to me using him as a pillow, I appreciate him letting me sleep. Maybe he just had a rough day yesterday and he'll be a completely different person today. Or maybe he doesn't like traveling and now that we're here, he'll be in a better mood today. I can definitely hope. He reaches down on the side of his seat, pulling on the lever and raising his seat back. Then, he extends his hands up, linking his fingers together and flipping his wrists as he stretches his arms above his head, attempting to wake himself up and loosen his stiff muscles from having to sleep on the plane.

I take a deep breath and exhale slowly, before I hesitantly glance in his direction out of the corner of my eye. He runs his hands over his face, before dropping them into his lap with a heavy sigh. Mustering my courage, I force myself to turn and face him, hoping for better results. "Good morning," I murmur softly, smiling brightly at him.

He narrows his eyes slightly, giving me a look I can't quite decipher, and not saying a single word in response. Then, I watch as he reaches into his jeans pocket and pulls out a small, rectangular, silver tin full of breath mints. He opens it and pops one into his mouth, before he holds the open tin out towards me. "Have a mint," he insists.

My smile falters and my face instantly heats with embarrassment. I reach out and pinch a small, round, white mint between my fingers. Awkwardly, I mumble, "Thanks," before I immediately drop it into my mouth and snap it closed. Clasping the lid shut, he slips the tin back into his pocket. Then he turns away from me and raises the small window shade, brightening our space. Peering out the window to the water down below, he leans forward and twists his body, keeping his back towards me and successfully blocking my view. Frowning, I glare at his back, before I reluctantly fall back into my seat with a heavy sigh. I guess his mood isn't any better today. I shake my head, attempting to rid myself of any negativity. I tell myself I'm not about to let him, or anyone else for that matter, ruin my day or my vacation.

I unbuckle my seat belt and stand up, stretching my legs. I make my way to the bathroom at the front of the plane, knowing we're going to be landing soon. I wash my hands and dry them before I pull out my phone. I want to record another vlog, especially since I haven't been able to do as many updates as I'd hoped with my friendly seat neighbor.

Holding my phone up in front of me, I press record and grin back at my image. "Hey guys. Okay, so I'm in the restroom of the plane and that's because Mr. Personality sitting next to me didn't like that I was making videos in first class," I quietly retort, annoyed. I take a calming breath and exhale slowly before I continue. "But first class is amazing and I can't wait to tell you more about it," I declare with enthusiasm. "I'll see you in Malta! Bye," I state, grinning broadly. Then, I tap the red button on my screen to end the video.

I slip my phone into my pocket as I step out of the bathroom. Walking slowly, I make my way back to my seat, just as the speakers crackle to life. "Good morning, ladies and gentlemen," an announcement begins overhead. "We are just beginning our decent into Malta," she continues. "The temperature in Malta today will be a high of seventy two degrees. If you're here visiting, enjoy your stay and if you're returning home, welcome home. At this time, we ask that you please return to your seats, fasten your seatbelts, close your tray tables and return your seats to the upright and locked position. Please make sure all of your belongings are stowed safely under your seat, or in the overhead compartments. Our flight attendants are beginning to make their way through the cabin for one last compliance check and to collect any cups, wrappers, napkins and other trash, before taking their seats for the remainder of the flight. We will be on the ground shortly. Thank you for flying with us and we hope you'll fly with us again very soon."

I feel my excitement growing as I get settled back in my seat. I quickly do as the announcement instructed and buckle my seatbelt, as well as double check the levers, making sure my seat is as it should be. The same flight attendant who came through last night, steps up to our row with a polite smile. I don't know how she does it, probably getting very little sleep while attending to everyone. I'd be exhausted. "Any trash?" she inquires.

I grin back at her, appreciating her simple manners. At least she's been kind to me throughout the flight. I gesture to the rigid back of the grumpy man next to me and grumble sarcastically, "Does he count?"

He straightens and slowly turns towards me. He clenches his jaw as he looks at me through narrowed eyes, obviously offended. I flinch inwardly from his look alone, but maintain my relaxed demeanor. I don't know why I'm letting this man get to me so much that I make a rude comment, but I couldn't seem to stop myself. I don't even know this guy. I can't let him bother me. "Excuse me?" he questions, irritably.

"Nothing," I murmur. I paste a smile on my face and give him a slight shake of my head. I feel my stomach twist with a slight pang of regret. I remind myself that he's been incredibly rude on this long flight. I'm allowed to be irritated sometimes. He glares at me for a moment longer, as if daring me to repeat myself. I keep my lips pinched tightly together, refusing to comply. He finally slowly turns away from me and returns his attention to looking out the window at the view, the same view I wouldn't mind being able to see. The flight attendant gives me a comforting smile and a gentle pat on my shoulder. I grin back at her in appreciation, before she continues on down the aisle to the rest of the passengers.

Soon, even the flight attendants have taken their seats and buckled themselves in. Since I'm not able to even glance out the window next to me, I look across the plane and catch a glimpse of water in various shades of blues and even greens, just before I see a few rock formations popping out of the waters. Soon, I spy an array of colors and shapes in a blur, before gradually coming into focus, as we approach the ground. I grip the armrests of my seat, my heart racing in anticipation as I smile wide. I'm so excited to get my vacation started. I do wish Kristen were here with me like we planned, but I refuse to dwell on what could've been and let it ruin my trip. I'm going to be sure to make the best out of every single moment I'm here in Malta. I may never have another opportunity to be able to go on a trip like this.

Thankfully, my ears pop, just before we touch the ground, relieving the effects from the changes in air pressure and allowing me to really hear well again. I feel the small jolt of the plane as the wheels first come into contact with the ground. I'm pushed gently back in my seat, as the pilot hits the brakes, a dulled sound of them screeching to a halt rings in my ears as we come to a near stop towards the end of the runway. I grin and clap along with most of the other passengers on the plane in appreciation for the safe flight, but of course the man next to me just heaves another heavy sigh. Oh, well. It's not like I'll ever see him again, anyway. It's time to push this man and his negativity out of my thoughts and start enjoying my vacation.

I anxiously wait my turn as everyone exits row by row. I stand up, grabbing my things and then follow the people in front of me towards the exit. As I step off the plane, I instantly feel a wall of warmer air. I grin, appreciating being away from the cold winter of New York. I step to the side and out of the way, allowing other passengers to exit the plane while I wait. I need to stay here to collect my bags, since I had to check in at the gate so late. It doesn't take long before a tall gentleman with black hair and lightly tanned skin dressed in a uniform from the airline steps up to me and hands me my bags with a broad, friendly smile. "Welcome to Malta," he greets me.

"Thank you," I grin, feeling my excitement growing by the second. I grasp my bags and quickly rearrange them to make them easier to carry. Then, I spin on my heel, offering the gentleman one more smile over my shoulder. I make my way through the bright airport, stopping at the sign of the first women's restroom I see.

After using the restroom, I wash my hands and look at myself in the mirror. I look like I slept in my clothes last night, but I don't care. I giggle, my anticipation increasing every moment. I smooth down my hair, mostly still pulled back in its braid and apply some pale pink lip-gloss, before smiling back at my reflection. It's definitely not perfect, but it's perfect for me and for right now. I can't believe I'm really here!

I grin and reach into my pocket, pulling out my phone. Holding it up in front of me for another quick video while I have the chance, I press record. I cheerfully begin, "Hey everyone! I made it! Here I am in Malta," I broadcast, my giddiness obvious. "The airport is in a city named Guda, or Gudja, or something like that," I stammer awkwardly and shake my head at myself. "Needless to say it was a long flight, especially sitting next to that lovely seat partner of mine. But besides him, I did enjoy first class and I'm sorry I didn't get to share everything with you guys, but I'm here! Yes, it's raining here, but after every storm comes a rainbow. Right?" I prompt, maintaining my positivity. "I'm not going to let a little bit of rain get me down," I assert. "So, I have an hour or so drive up to my hotel, located right on the coast," I emphasize. "So, follow my adventures as I travel around Malta," I encourage. Ciao!" I happily declare. I blow a kiss towards my screen and tap my phone to end the video.

I quickly upload the video and then take a moment to play it back, watching to see how it turned out. I chuckle, noticing a delay between the video images and my words, probably from my stellar international service. "Oh, well," I murmur, shrugging my shoulders. It's not like I can do anything to help right now and I refuse to let anything bother me.

I find the customs line relatively short and easily make my way through. Now, I can go find my shuttle, so I can make my way to my resort, Ramla Bay. I can't wait to get there! In the meantime, I'll enjoy the scenery on the ride over. I wouldn't be able to wipe the smile from my face if I wanted to as I follow the signs to my destination.

Making my way to the front of the airport, I bypass baggage claim, with my suitcases already at my side and look around, searching for the sign for my ride. Instead, I turn and suddenly spot my friendly seat partner rolling two large suitcases through the airport, one black and one dark blue with yellow trim. Maybe I should attempt to talk to him one more time. If not for anything else, I would at least like to ask him to pass on a thank you to his friend that gave me his seat. After everything, I would've been heartbroken not to be able to get on the plane.

Chapter 5

Michael

I step out of the plane and quickly stride past the beautiful, but annoyingly cheerful woman who sat next to me as she waits for the suitcase she checked in at the last minute. I heave a sigh and make my way to the carousel to collect my luggage. As I wait for the suitcases to start dropping down onto the belt, I pull out my phone and turn it on. I notice several missed texts and two missed calls. I check the texts and see one from Daryl. I tap to open it and read, "I wasn't able to get my suitcase off in time. Can you please bring it home for me?" he requests. "Thank you!" he adds, knowing I won't be able to respond until we land.

"Great!" I grumble. Just then the belt starts moving and Daryl's navy blue suitcase, accented with yellow piping falls down the ramp first. I reach down and yank it off, before setting it next to me. Gratefully, only a few bags later, I swipe my black suitcase off the belt. Grasping one suitcase in each hand, I roll them behind me towards customs. After I'm through, I hear a soft, sweet voice call out, "Hey." But I don't know anyone here, so I keep walking. Then I see her out of the corner of my eye, looking right at me. "Hey, 9C. I'm talking to you," she declares.

Turning, I glance back at her over my right shoulder. I arch my eyebrow in question, "Me?"

She nods her head and confirms, "Yes."

I slow down so she can catch up with me. Then I probe, "9C?"

The corners of her mouth twitch up in amusement, but she answers matter of fact. "That's the seat you were in," she states. "You never told me your name."

"Oh," I acknowledge.

"Excuse me?" she prompts, irritably.

I don't know why I keep pushing her buttons. I don't even know this woman, but I can't seem to help myself. I finally come to a stop and really look at her. I'm instantly thrown a little off balance at the sight of her. Her soft, brown hair is falling out of her braid and her toffee brown eyes appear tired, but bright. It's hard to believe she looks this stunning after all those hours on a plane, including sleeping. "What do you want?" I provoke, petulantly.

She looks slightly taken aback by my tone and I fight a visible cringe, not happy with my own reaction. "I just wanted to say thank you, all right?" she prods. I appreciate your brother giving me that seat. I meant to tell you that he wants you to get his bags."

"This?" I say and nod towards the bags in my hands. I look at her and arch my eyebrows in challenge, even though she couldn't have known one of these suitcases was his. She forces a smile and nods her head in response. I sigh, disappointed with my own attitude, but I can't stop myself.

"Right," she mumbles. "Well, I hope you have a great time," she says, maintaining her kind demeanor. "I've never been to Malta," she adds.

"Neither have I," I grumble. "And I was supposed to come for the first time with my brother," I inform her.

"It seems like he didn't want to go on the trip to begin with," she claims.

I flinch at her comment. I narrow my eyes and insist, "You have no idea what you're talking about." He'd be on this plane on his way to Malta with the woman who was supposed to be his wife, if he had a choice. I can't say I'm not happy they're not together anymore, but I do wish they broke up sooner. He doesn't deserve so much heartbreak. No one does, but Daryl is a good man and an even better brother. I'm going to say something I regret if I continue standing here with her. I turn away from her and start to walk away. I hear her call after me, her sarcasm thick, "Merry Christmas to you, too!"

I huff a humorless laugh, knowing she's probably calling me a jerk under her breath and I couldn't even blame her. I pick up my pace and quickly make my way out of the airport, surprised by the warm, but incredibly mild weather. I guess I just assumed it was hot, like the Caribbean, but this is nice, I admit to myself.

I notice the signs for various hotels and resorts and find the one I'm looking for just as a shuttle pulls up. The driver steps out of the van, appearing to be a couple years older than me and about an inch shorter. He has short brown hair, brown eyes, an oval face and a broad build. He's dressed in black pants and a plain white button down shirt with a nametag pinned to the front of his shirt. "Hello, everyone and welcome," he greets us with an accent. "I'll be your driver over to the resort. Please feel free to ask me any questions on the short drive," he offers. "It should only take us about ten to fifteen minutes," he advises.

I hear several people mumble, "Thank you," as I patiently wait my turn. A young couple hands the driver their luggage and climbs in, moving to the last row of the van, while he loads their things into the back. Next, a tall, thin gentleman with gray hair does the same for both him and his wife, a petite woman with short gray hair nearly a foot shorter than her husband and blue eyes. He helps her inside the van and they slide into the middle row. The last couple in front of me is a good-looking, black couple. The man has short black hair, brown eyes, broad shoulders and a square jaw. He looks adoringly down at his wife, with her straight brown hair, golden eyes and angelic looking skin and immediately offers her the front seat. When the driver gets to me, I hand him my suitcase and climb inside. I sit down on the black leather bench seat in the front, right next to the gentleman who just climbed in.

Just as the driver is about to close the door behind me, I hear the same soft voice I've been listening to all night. "Wait! Wait for me!" she yells. I ignore the tightening in my chest and bite the inside of my cheek, fighting any further reaction.

"Let me help you with that," the driver instantly offers. He rushes towards her with a broad smile.

He takes the suitcase from her and she smiles at him in appreciation. "Thank you so much," she proclaims.

"You're welcome," he replies. He makes his way to the back of the van and loads her suitcase inside, along with the rest of our bags.

"It's nice to know chivalry isn't dead yet," she comments. Of course she likes that stuff. She steps into my view after the driver loads her suitcase and winces at the sight of me. I roll my eyes in annoyance at her reaction. She stands staring at me and I realize my backpack is sitting in the last remaining seat. Of course the only place for her to sit is next to me. I huff in annoyance and reluctantly scoot over to make room for her.

She forces a smile and mumbles, "Thank you." I don't bother responding. I know she wishes I were anywhere else, but here. I instantly see the irritation on her face. "You know, decent human beings usually respond with, 'You're welcome.'"

I turn and glare at her. She thinks she can just give me a lesson on manners? No way. I'm obviously dealing with more important things at the moment than entertaining a beautiful stranger. Instead of saying thank you, like I know I should, I respond with sarcasm. "Who ever said I was a decent human being?" I question.

She gasps and her mouth drops open, her surprise at my response evident. She opens her mouth to say something, but then snaps it closed, before doing it again, reminding me of a fish, blindly searching for food. I turn away from her and look out the window, as I reach into my pocket for my headphones. I slip them into my ears and reach for my sunglasses, immediately putting them on, while I unsuccessfully attempt to ignore the woman with her side pressed against mine.

It's not until we drive away from the airport that I realize he's driving on the left side of the road making me thankful I'm not the one driving. We pass by some farmland and trees, before we make our way through town, passing several buildings, restaurants and shops. I barely notice the architecture or the people, my thoughts still focused on my family.

I breathe a sigh of relief, as we pull through large wrought iron gates, attached to a pale stone wall. I need some space from people right now. Mostly, I need space from the woman sitting right next to me, with a gorgeous smile on her face. She's practically radiating happiness and excitement. This must be the resort. The van drives around and stops in front of a paver walkway in various shades of tan and gray, leading to the front of the hotel. In the middle of the walkway sits a beautiful round, four-tiered fountain that appears to be a brushed bronze, with paths in four different directions. Along the paths are perfectly landscaped gardens, with green bushes, plants and flowers in reds, whites and purples. I pull my headphones out of my ears and slip them into my pocket, anxious to unload everything in my room. I can't wait to sleep in a real bed tonight.

The woman next to me doesn't move to get out of the van, instead she looks around, taking in her surroundings. I groan in irritation. I'm not in the mood to wait for her to have some manners. I decide I'm not going to wait for her. I climb over her and immediately step out of the van with my backpack slung over my shoulder. I take a deep breath, the scent of salt water in the air. I glance to the right and beyond, but see nothing but rows and rows of grapes. This must be a winery too. I was just so focused on supporting my brother that I didn't even bother to look into where I was going. I squint into the sun on my left, searching for the source of the salt water, but I just see more of the resort in that direction. The front of the hotel has a beautiful pale stone front, similar to the pillars at the entrance. The first building is an L shape, with the shorter end pointing towards the entrance to my left, with very few windows. The front door is located in the middle of the longer side of the building. It has black, wooden, double doors, with a small balcony, encased by a white railing, perched atop. To the left is a porch with three, tall, white columns, the Italian influence of the architecture reminding me of where I am. To my right, the building has only windows to take in the view. The windows all have a rounded hood, accented with white grilles. I have to admit, this place is incredibly beautiful. I heave a sigh, wishing I had someone to share it with and then remind myself this is supposed to be my brother's honeymoon. Why am I here?

I turn and as the men help their wives and the driver moves to the woman's side, helping her as she struggles with her bags, I grind my jaw impatiently. I grab my wallet out of my pocket and pull out a couple dollars. I quickly tip the driver, before he gets ahold of her suitcase.

Then I grab both Daryl's suitcase and mine. I grumble, "Thanks," under my breath, not even sure he heard me. I swiftly make my way past the other passengers, including the woman who seems to continue invading my space, keeping my focus in front of me.

I stride into the front lobby, dragging the suitcases behind me over the dark mahogany wood floors. I grimace at the Christmas decorations all around the lobby, quickly striding through on my way to the desk. I pass by small square tables and chairs in a dark wood, keeping my focus straight ahead. Along the edges, several lights hang down from the ceiling, looking like elaborate wrought iron sconces encasing four light bulbs. Smaller versions are hung on the walls near the doors as actual sconces. The walls are painted white with wainscoting on the bottom and detailed crown moldings up above. A wall of white bricks encases the windows on the far end of the room. Those windows appear to sink into the wall and push out further for a better view of the landscaping. The wall to my right is lined with windows trimmed with a pale wood, all overlooking the vineyard. I walk up to the desk, the front of it is covered with thin quarter-inch gray and white tiles about four inches long and staggered to give it texture. A white and gray swirled granite desktop completes the look.

"Michael Foster," I announce, instantly providing the desk clerk with my name as I hand over my credit card for incidentals.

He smiles politely at me and greets me, "Welcome to Ramla Bay." I stare, barely paying attention to his friendly greeting in his thick accent. He's a few inches shorter than me with light brown skin, an oval face, curly black hair and brown eyes. He's wearing what I assume to be the hotel uniform, a tan button up shirt with a nametag pinned to his chest. He pulls me up in the computer and begins typing away. I stand stiffly, just waiting for him to hand over my room key. I breathe a sigh of relief as he hands me my key and returns my credit card before giving me directions to my room.

I spin around and stride for the exit, attempting to ignore the woman and the other passengers from the van as they walk into the lobby for check-in. I quickly make my way to my room. I'm anxious to get everything unpacked and throw Daryl's suitcase in the corner until I go home. My stomach growls loudly as I reach my door. I grimace and glare at my stomach. I probably should've eaten something on the plane. Now, I'm tired and hungry. I sigh heavily. "This is going to be a long couple weeks," I grumble to myself, again wondering why I came.

I open the door and push inside, dragging the suitcases behind me. It's a big room. Then again, this was supposed to be Daryl's honeymoon suite. There's a seating area when I walk in with a black leather couch and chair, end tables on each side of the couch and a rectangular dark wood coffee table. Jutting out from the wall in the middle of the room sits a desk and next to it lays a long table filled with items, separating the two sides of the room. I walk further into the room and drop my suitcases. I find a large walk-in closet on my right, along with a full bathroom and a separate vanity area. Then on my left is a king sized bed with an embroidered white quilt and several pillows on top near the thick and detailed cherry wood rounded headboard. In the middle of the bed, sits two white towels rolled together in the shape of a swan with their beaks forming a heart as they kiss in the middle. A third towel forms another heart in front of the swans and it's accented with red roses on each side. There's a nightstand on each side of the bed and a TV enclosed in an armoire at the end of the bed. On the other side of the bed there's sliding glass doors. I peek

49

through the glass and see a nice size balcony overlooking the resort, Malta and my first glimpse of the salt water.

I drop down on the corner of the bed and glance at the table. I grimace, realizing it's all of Daryl's honeymoon extras left for him and Beverly. A beautiful bouquet of both red and white roses sits in a vase next to a huge wicker basket full of fresh fruit and other treats. Next to the basket lays a green glass bottle sitting on ice, the top wrapped with gold foil. I pull it out and glance at the label. "Champagne, of course," I mumble. Two clear champagne glasses with the name of the resort etched into the glass and the year, sits next to the bottle. I notice a small white card propped on the table. I reach for it and flip it open.

I begin reading, glaring at the card from the staff here at the resort. "Congratulations on your wedding! Enjoy your time here and our special gifts. Please keep the glasses as a wedding gift from us." I shake my head, my heart aching once again for my brother.

Chapter 6

Shea

I can't believe how rude 9C has been since the moment I met him! Now he climbs over me to get out of the van as fast as he can. Then he just pushes past everyone like we're not important or like the van is on fire and he only cares about saving himself. What is wrong with this guy? I watch him walk away, stalking inside the hotel, while I continue to struggle with my suitcase. I shake my head in annoyance, trying to push him out of my mind again. Of course he's staying at the same resort as me. I mumble to myself, reiterating, "I'm in Malta. It's time to enjoy myself, not fret about a handsome jerk I don't even know."

The driver approaches me with a kind smile and immediately reaches towards my suitcase offering, "Let me help you."

I breathe a sigh of relief and grin up at him in appreciation. "Thank you so much," I murmur, as he tugs it free for me. I reach into my purse and pull out my wallet. I grab a ten-dollar bill and drop my wallet back into my purse. I glance up, an apologetic look on my face. "I'm sorry, but all I have is American money," I inform him, holding it out in appreciation.

He reaches out and takes it from me with a wide grin. "Grazzi. Thank you. Have a beautiful trip. Il-Milied it-tajjeb," he declares.

My eyebrows draw down in confusion, as I attempt to decipher the meaning of his words. "Excuse me?" I ask for clarification.

He chuckles softly and responds. "That means, 'Merry Christmas' in my language of Maltese," he explains.

"Il-Milied it-tajjeb," I repeat, brokenly in attempt to echo the saying.

His smile grows and he praises me for my efforts. "Good! Very good," he proclaims.

"Grazzi," I reply, proud of myself. I return his smile and he tips his head towards me in response. Then he makes his way around the van and slides back in behind the wheel. I spin around and face the front of the resort. It's absolutely gorgeous and the Christmas decorations make it look even more spectacular, if that's possible. The building is expansive, reminding me of an old-fashioned estate from the south. It's made of stone in shades of gray with a black roof, and white trim, including massive white poles holding up the overhead of the portico. Thick garland wraps around all the white columns of the exterior and then it's draped from one pole to the next. I wouldn't be surprised to find it all lit up with lights at night. There's a large wreath on the front door, wrapped with a thick red velvet ribbon and decorated with pinecones and red berries. I notice a Christmas tree in the corner where the building turns at a ninety-degree angle, extending towards me, along with two other trees, one on each end and all of them appear to be decorated.

I smile as I walk inside, stepping through the front door. I look around, taking in all the beautiful architecture and Christmas decorations. I tilt my head back, glancing up to a beautiful domed ceiling letting in the sunlight, the skylights appearing like a grid in the dome. I return my gaze in front of me, glancing around at all the gold and silver glittery snowflakes scattered around the walls in the room. I make my way across the lobby and step towards the front desk.

I notice 9C standing with the desk clerk, so I stop and patiently wait in line. I look around the room, appreciating the decorations, while I wait my turn. The front of the desk has gold garland sweeping across the front edge, with red velvet bows attached at the end. A simple gold roping with tassels on the ends adorns the windows and doors, along with glittery snowflakes on the upper corners. Signs in silver and gold, wishing everyone a Merry Christmas hang behind the desk as well as one on each wall. A wreath made of gold entwined branches wrapped with a silver ribbon and tied with a silver bow hangs on the wall just to the right of the desk. This is definitely a room full of silver and gold.

The guy from 9C strides by me, peering right over my head, as if I don't exist. I narrow my eyes in irritation, but he never even bothers to look my way.

"May I help the next guest, please?" the desk clerk calls out.

Tearing my gaze away from his retreating back, I take a deep breath and walk up to the desk with a huge smile. I don't want to take my annoyance with 9C out on the desk clerk. "Hi!" I greet him cheerfully.

"Hello! Welcome," he replies.

"Thank you. I have a reservation under Shea Andrews," I inform him.

He taps away at the computer in front of him. He soon nods his head in acknowledgement and smiles. "Ah, yes, right here," he mumbles. He turns and looks back at me. "May I have your credit card for incidentals?" he requests.

"Yes, certainly," I mumble, nodding my head in agreement. I look down and reach into my purse, grabbing my wallet again. Flipping it open, I pull out my credit card and hand it to over the counter to the clerk.

He takes it and scans it into the computer. "Thank you," he declares. "There's a complimentary cocktail hour in the hotel bar at five this evening, should you like to join us," he enlightens me, as we wait for my card to process.

"That sounds wonderful," I admit.

He hands me back my credit card, along with my room key. Then he reaches behind him and picks up a huge wicker basket filled with all kinds of goodies. My eyes widen in surprise as he hands it to me over the desk. "What is this?" I ask.

He grins and proudly reveals, "Your friend arranged it for you."

My mouth drops slightly open and I gasp in surprise as I peek to see what's inside. There's popcorn, chocolates, fruit, trail mix, granola, two bottles of wine, two wine glasses, along with a bunch of other treats. "Thank you," I tell him. I'm not sure if Kristen left this for me because she feels guilty or not, but either way this is an incredibly generous gift.

"You are in a panoramic suite, number four-thirty-two," he informs me. "The easiest way to your room would be for you to take the stairs behind you to the second floor, make a right and there's an elevator on your left down the short hallway. Take that up to the fourth floor, go to your right and you are all the way at the end of the hallway on the right hand side," he instructs.

"Thank you so much," I repeat, picturing the directions in my head to help me remember.

"You are welcome," he replies. "Enjoy your stay."

"Grazzi!" I reiterate. "Il-Milied it-tajjeb!" I declare.

He brightens and starts speaking to me in Maltese. "Ma kontx naf li titkellem bil-Malti! Qatt ma sibt Amerikan li jaf il-lingwa taghna," he proclaims.

My eyes widen to the size of saucers. I don't understand a single word he just said. I shake my head

54

and smile, attempting to appear both apologetic and polite. "Oh, no, no, no," I stammer awkwardly. "I don't speak Maltese. I'm sorry," I emphasize.

I notice his eyes fill with disappointment and I can't help but feel bad. "Oh. Okay," he replies, poorly hiding his disappointment. "Enjoy your stay," he repeats.

I feel my face heat with embarrassment and I give him another look of apology. Then, I paste on the brightest smile I can muster, hoping I don't come off looking too ridiculous. "Thank you," I accentuate.

He nods in acknowledgement and then turns to the next person in line. "May I help the next guest, please?" he requests. The couple that sat behind me in the van steps up to the desk, as I drag my suitcase away.

I take the stairs as he suggested and find the elevator, before I make my way all the way down the hall to my room at the end. I set my luggage aside as I unlock the door. I grasp my things as I push my way into the room and grin, happy to finally be here. I glance around in appreciation and mumble to myself, "This is perfect."

There's a full bath to my right as soon as I walk in and a nice sized closet on my left with mirrors on the front of the doors. I'll appreciate the full length later on when I'm getting ready for dinner. Just past the closet I find a locked door that I assume leads to another guest room. Next to that sits a long dresser, an armoire with a television inside followed by a desk. There are two queen size beds, both with a beautiful white embroidered quilt and a red decorative pillow, giving the room the perfect splash of color. Then between the two beds sits a nightstand with an alarm clock, a resort phone and a charging station for my cellphone. On the far side of the room, near the corner, there's a small round table with two chairs. Behind the table, there's a sliding glass door, leading out onto a good-sized balcony overlooking the resort, Malta and the water beyond. I smile to myself, genuinely happy I decided to come alone. I would have regretted it if I didn't make the trip. I'm going to make sure to take advantage of my time while I'm here.

I make my way over to my suitcase and awkwardly heave it up onto the bed furthest from the balcony doors, barely maintaining my balance. I unzip it and flip it open, surprised by how everything appears to be almost exactly as I packed it. I thought it would move around a bit more, especially with the long flight. I pick up a red dress and immediately hang it up in the closet. I may still have a few wrinkles, but the faster I unpack, the less I'll have to do later to make it look good. I go back to my suitcase and pick up a pile of shorts. I spin around and open the bottom drawer of the dresser and place the pile inside. I turn back to my suitcase and swiftly finish unpacking all of my clothes, shoes, accessories and putting them away. Then, I grab my bathroom bag and do the same with all of those items. I zip up my suitcase and put it into the back of the closet, before I close the door, feeling a sense of both satisfaction and accomplishment.

I smile to myself as I sit down at the end of the bed closest to the balcony. Sighing happily, I flop onto my back and glance out the sliding glass door with a huge smile on my face. There's so much I want to do and see while I'm here. I can't wait to go exploring. Not today though. Today I want to relax, eat some dinner, maybe have a drink and take my time checking out where I'll be staying the next couple of weeks.

I roll over onto my stomach and reach down to my purse. I stick my hand in and grasp onto a smooth piece of paper and pull out one of the brochures for Malta. I read through it again, for probably the tenth time since I left the states. Malta is an island-state off the southern most tip of Sicily in the Mediterranean Sea. It consists of three islands, Malta being the largest, although it is the smallest country in Europe. It has become a main freight transshipment point, a financial center and a popular tourist destination with all its history. I love being able to learn about the place I'm visiting. I think it helps me appreciate it even more.

I continue on, glancing at some of the different places I want to visit. I definitely want to see the old capital of Mdina. There's supposed to be some spectacular views from the Upper Barrakka Gardens. Then the San Anton Gardens are believed to be incredible too. I won't be doing any diving, so I can skip those parts. I'd like to see the temples. I definitely want to visit the Mosta Dome and St. John's Co-Cathedral, especially the marble tombstone floor meant to honor the knights there. The stories I've been reading have completely captured my attention. I'd like to visit the fishing village and I definitely want to spend a lot of time at the Valletta Waterfront to eat, go shopping, and maybe even check out the nightlife there. I glance down at the picture of the Azure window. It's a natural rock arch coming out of the sea and connecting to a cliff. It was created by the collapse of a sea cave. Then, it unfortunately collapsed during a storm in 2017, but people still flock to it for the views, diving and cliff jumping. I wince just thinking about cliff jumping off of a 92-foot rock formation, but more because of landing in the water than the jump itself. There's no way I'm going in water over my head, but it's an absolute must to see with its history! I do think it's incredibly sad the formation is not completely there anymore, but it makes me wonder how long it will be before mother nature decides to change the land formation again.

Suddenly, I realize I haven't texted Kristen yet and I promised to let her know as soon as I made it here safe. I immediately drop the brochure and sit up, pulling my phone out of my pocket. I don't want her to worry. I unlock the screen and quickly scroll to her name. Then, I swiftly type out a message. "I made it. It's beautiful here. You're really missing out," I declare. I pause and bite my bottom lip, wondering if I should send it like this. I don't want her to feel bad about not coming, but I also want her to know I do wish she were here with me. This was supposed to be a trip with my best friend, but after all the time we spent planning and anticipating this trip, I'm here alone instead. I take a deep breath and tap send, without regret. Then, I drop the phone down on the bed and turn to look out the window again.

Chapter 7

Michael

"I made it. It's beautiful here. You're really missing out," I tap out the message on my phone to Daryl. I stare at the text momentarily, before I hit send. I heave a sigh, trying not to overthink everything, but at the moment, that's easier said than done. I drop my phone onto the nightstand, not bothering to wait for his response. I still can't believe I'm on his honeymoon without him. Then again, this trip is probably the last place I would want to be if I were in his position. I don't blame him. I just question whether or not I should be here. I'm only on this vacation because I wanted to be here for my brother after everything he's been through with her and now he's back home with the rest of our family, while I'm here alone. Why did I let him talk me into this? I shake my head and attempt to push my negative thoughts out of my mind.

I kick off my shoes and socks and walk over to the sliding glass door. I pull it open and step out onto the balcony. There's a pale gray stone wall that divides each balcony. It angles down as it gets closer to the end of the balcony, giving me privacy and also allowing me to see more of the view. Instead of a normal iron railing, there's thick, clear Plexiglas, so I'm able to look out at an unobstructed view of Malta. I step towards it and fold my arms on the top of the rail framing the glass. I lean down with another sigh and look out at what my view will be for the next two weeks. Just below me, I'm overlooking part of the resort. I'm able to see the edge of the vineyards, but they must be mostly around the other side. I'm looking down on two large pools surrounded by tables, chairs and lounges with guests and employees milling about. The pool further away appears to be an oval shape, following the curve of the island. Just beyond the oval pool lays an area with numerous lounges and a spectacular, peaceful cove, with various types and sizes of boats anchored off the island. On the water, along the other side of the cove, sits a large, white building in a crescent shape. It appears to be another hotel or resort with all the windows and balconies. The rest of the land appears to be town, residences and simple, but beautiful landscaping. Just beyond the cove, I glance out at the open sea, watching as small waves crest and fall as they near the island.

I take a deep breath, the scent of salt water now prevalent. I have to admit, I'm starting to feel a little more relaxed as I take in the scenery, but I can't exactly sit here and do nothing for two weeks. The thought reminds me that Daryl has a whole itinerary of activities and reservations he transferred over to me too. I shouldn't let all of that go to waste, but doing all those things he planned for two by myself doesn't feel quite right either.

I spot a Christmas tree down below and take another deep breath, slowly exhaling the fresh air. It sure doesn't feel like Christmas. "What am I supposed to do?" I grumble to myself. My stomach growls loudly, as if giving me an answer, at least one for right now. I stand and spin around sauntering back into the room, sliding the door closed behind me.

I walk over and grab a dark red apple out of the fruit basket. Picking it up, I take a large bite, my teeth crunching into the sweet fruit. I glance at my suitcase laying open on the bed, everything still packed neatly inside. I guess I'll unpack and get settled. Then, I can jump in the shower and change into something more appropriate for dinner.

It doesn't take me long to put all my things away into the dresser and clean myself up. The shower did help wake me up. I'm beginning to feel a little bit more like myself, but I'm still struggling with being here alone, albeit at all, especially for the holidays. Maybe going to get a drink before I grab some dinner will help me feel more like I'm on vacation. I pull on a pair of nice, dark, skinny jeans, a casual, short-sleeved, steel blue button down shirt and a pair of brown loafers. I glance in the mirror and run my hand over the top of my hair, patting down a few stray hairs. Then I grab my room key, my wallet and my phone, slipping everything in my pockets before I walk out the door. I make my way down to the hotel bar and restaurant, which I believe is the resort's more casual dining. I did notice on the information the guy at the front desk gave me, that they have some outdoor dining areas by the pools, as well as another by the vineyard and a more upscale restaurant inside overlooking the vineyard as well.

I take a step inside and look around, taking in my surroundings. The floors are a medium oak, similar to the large, square bar top in the center of the room. Wide plank, dark walnut, high top tables are scattered around the perimeter of the room, with four backless bar stools at each table with a cushioned black leather seat. Then, bar stools are placed all around the bar, minus the opening where the bartender and other employees go in and out. In the far corner there's a small station with a computer for the wait staff to put in orders and enter the customers payments for their bills. The walls are a light tan with beautiful white baseboards, chair moldings and crown moldings, accented with simple red and white Christmas decorations.

On the other side of the room, right in the center, there's a comfortable seating area with a black leather couch, love seat and two chairs, along with a square, dark wood coffee table in between. It faces a large wall with thin tiles, the coloring similar to the exterior of the building. In the middle of the wall sits a beautiful, long, two-sided electric fireplace, with red and white Christmas stockings hanging from the mantle below and a large television mounted above it. On both sides of the wall are two sets of French doors draped with garland, leading out to a patio, with a third set around the corner on both the left and the right, giving easy access to the outdoors. Elegant wrought iron tables and chairs with dark green umbrellas, sit on the patio overlooking a section of the winery.

"You can have a seat anywhere you'd like," a woman informs me, interrupting my perusal. I glance in the direction the voice came from and barely nod my head in acknowledgement. She's wearing a tan button-down shirt and slim black pants, similar to the man's uniform from the desk. She has long, smooth, ebony hair, dark chocolate eyes and tanned flawless skin. She folds her hands in front of her and looks up at me with a polite smile I don't bother returning.

I turn and walk away, passing by couples of all ages having a drink, eating dinner, talking and laughing as I make my way around the left side of the bar. Everyone here seems to be having a good time, the observation only making me feel more alone and frustrated. I sigh heavily as I lower myself onto a barstool, leaning my arms on the bar.

The bartender immediately strides over to me as he dries his hands on a small white hand towel, before he drops it underneath the bar. He steps up to me and offers me a wide smile. His smile would be contagious if I wasn't in such a bad mood, but I can't seem to drag myself out of this state of mind. "Hello!" he cheerfully greets me. I bite my tongue, reminding myself not to take my irritation out on him. "What can I get for you, Sir?" he inquires.

He seems to be close in age to my dad and about the same height as me. He has broad shoulders, dark chocolate brown skin, gentle brown eyes and short, tightly curled dark hair. He's wearing the same tan button down shirt as the other employees, with a resort nametag, stating his name is Sam. "Could I please have a pint of beer of whatever you have on tap?" I request, nodding towards the beer taps. "And a menu," I add. I glance up at the television above the bar, as my way of letting him know I'm done talking.

He nods his head in acknowledgement. Reaching underneath the bar, he pulls out a menu, handing it to me over the bar. Then, he makes his way down the bar, grabbing a clear glass beer mug and easily filling it up with minimal foam. He steps back over to me and places a cocktail napkin down with the resort name in black before setting the full mug down in front of me. "Let me know if you need anything," he urges, kindly. Then, he turns and saunters over to help another guest seated on the other side of the bar.

I take a drink of my beer, barely glancing at the menu. I feel like I'm too tired to do much of anything, although I know I should eat something. I take another sip of my beer and return it to the bar, continuing to stare at the TV, but not really processing the soccer game I'm watching. After barely a few minutes, I suddenly inhale the soft scent of her perfume as she lowers herself onto the stool next to me. My body instantly warms and tenses, knowing exactly who occupied the seat before I even glance in her direction. My eyes veer to her almost involuntarily. I can't help but watch as she looks around the room, smiling wide. She obviously didn't notice whom she was sitting down next to. I force my gaze to return to

63

the television, but I can't seem to stop watching her out of the corner of my eye, anticipating her reaction to seeing me.

The bartender approaches her with his welcoming smile and greets her. "Good evening, Miss. I'm Sam. What can I get you this evening?" he prompts.

"Surprise me," she declares, sounding almost giddy. "I'm on vacation," she proudly broadcasts. He laughs, a deep belly laugh as he nods in acknowledgement. Turning around, he makes his way down the bar and immediately begins making her a drink.

She sighs happily and continues taking in her surroundings. I feel it the moment her eyes land on me. I brace, anticipating a rude comment after my behavior towards her both last night and today, but she takes me by surprise. "Nine-C," she chimes. "How nice to see you here," she proclaims, with false sincerity.

"Ha-ha," I grumble. "Very funny."

She pauses, glancing around before she again attempts to start up a conversation with me. "It looks like you and I are the only singles here," she comments.

I quickly scan the room, again taking in all the couples and grimace. "Yeah and I'd like to keep it that way," I mutter in annoyance, as I return my stare to the television. I grind my jaw, wondering what possessed me to say that to this woman. I really am a jerk. My mom would be completely mortified, but I just couldn't help myself, my mind still stuck on what happened to my brother.

"What is that supposed to mean?" she demands, defiantly. She sounds irritated for the first time and I have an odd sense of accomplishment, making me even more disgusted with myself. Little does she know, I'm agreeing with her assessment of me on the inside, but I think my behavior proves she doesn't need to be around my negativity.

I feel the heat of her narrowed gaze on me without even turning my head. I cross my arms in front of me and lean on the bar top, as I attempt to ignore her, although I'm extremely aware she's sitting next to me. How could I not be? She looks incredibly beautiful in a thin, blush, sleeveless, mock turtleneck sweater dress. She's wearing her silky, long, brown hair down; now, hanging loose over her shoulders and her bright brown eyes could easily pull anyone's attention.

She opens her mouth to say something else to me, when Sam approaches and sets a glass with a short stem and a rounded globe down in front of her, interrupting my well-deserved scolding. The drink is a cherry red in color, with a wedge of pineapple and a round slice of orange sitting on the rim, next to a small, colorful, paper umbrella, with two maraschino cherries speared on the end. "Here you are," Sam announces, proudly.

"What's this?" she probes, curious. She reaches towards the drink and carefully pulls it closer to her across the bar.

"It's our national drink, The Maltese Falcon," he proudly informs her.

She giggles in response, while I fight my own smirk at the name and his claim. "Like the movie?" she questions.

"Exactly!" he proclaims, nodding his head firmly in confirmation.

I tilt my head towards him and arch my eyebrows in challenge. "You know, 'The Maltese Falcon' takes place in San Francisco, right?" I prod.

Sam's eyebrows draw down in confusion and he shakes his head in denial. "No, it's Malta. Like the title," he asserts, his smile returning.

"Have you ever seen it?" I inquire.

His face falls again and he shrugs his shoulders. "Well, ah, no," he admits, awkwardly, rubbing his hand along the back of his neck.

Out of the corner of my eye, I notice her scramble to pick up the drink in front of her and quickly take a sip. Then she sets it down and grins at Sam. She immediately interrupts, before either of us can say anything else. "Wow!" she exclaims. "This is delicious," she compliments.

Sam's whole face lights up with glee as he grins proudly. "Yes?" he prompts. "You like?" he questions, enjoying the praise.

"I do," she confirms, with a nod of her head.

"What's in it?" I question.

The woman narrows her eyes and glares at me again. "The, um, stuff dreams are made of," she stammers, answering for him. I bite the inside of my cheek, fighting back a smirk at her feistiness. I like it. Turning her attention back to Sam, she winks at him and places a Euro on the bar. Then, she stands and grabs her drink, before she spins on her heel and marches towards the back exit, leading out to the patio.

Sam turns towards me, his head tilted to the side, slightly puzzled. "Do you know what that means?" he inquires.

I drain the last of my beer and return the mug to the bar. Then, I reach into my pocket and pull out a Euro to pay for my drink. I place the money on the bar and nod my head in affirmation. "It's a line from the movie," I reveal.

He nods in understanding and glances after the woman, smiling. I plant my hands on the edge of the bar and push up from my seat. Then, I turn towards the front door and away from her, needing space before I say something I might regret even more. I walk around, checking out a little more of the resort, as I look for another place to eat dinner. I pass by several couples hand in hand, or arm in arm, just enjoying their time together in this remarkable location. I sigh heavily, making a decision based on my current state of mind. I'll just order something to eat from room service instead. I need to get out of here.

Chapter 8

Shea

I stride away from the man I call Nine-C like it's his given name, but what else should I call him when he doesn't bother introducing himself. I push the back door open, and step outside, closing the door softly behind me. Slowing my pace, I take a deep breath, appreciating the warm, fresh air, smelling of both salt as well as a little bit of sweet, like the grapes. Following the stone path right next to the building, I walk up to a small podium at the top of the trail. Pasting a smile on my face, I look up at a tall, slender young man, probably working his first job. He's slumping against the stand and straightens the moment he sees me coming. "Good evening, Miss," he greets me with a crooked smile and a thick accent.

"Hello," I respond politely. "Do you have any available tables out here tonight?" I request, hopeful.

He looks down and scrolls through an iPad in front of him. He lifts his gaze to mine and grins. "If you don't mind waiting for a few minutes, we should have an available table for you in just a little while," he offers.

"Thank you," I reply, grateful.

"You can wait just over there," he suggests. He holds his hand up gesturing towards a small seated area just off to the side including two over sized wicker chairs with ivory cushions and a matching loveseat and couch.

"Thank you," I repeat.

He nods his head in acknowledgement. I slowly spin on my heel, making my way over to a quiet space in the corner of the small section to wait for an open table. I really just want to be outside. I wouldn't be able to do this at home, especially at this time of year, so why not appreciate everything I can while I'm here?

Since it seems I have a few minutes before I'll be able to sit down at a table, I pull out my phone and hold it out in front of me, ready to do another update for my vlog. Taking a deep breath, I smile wide and press record. "Hey, guys!" I begin, "So, I'm here at the Ramla Bay Resort in Malayha," I pronounce hesitantly, hoping I'm saying it right. "And it's absolutely beautiful," I declare. "I'm taking full advantage of the warmer weather here. I'm currently waiting for an available table outside with a gorgeous view of the vineyard and the upcoming sunset."

I scrunch up my nose in apology and continue. "I'm sorry I didn't post earlier, but I guess I was a little jetlagged from the long flight and I fell asleep while I was unpacking. When I woke up, I barely had any time to get ready for the cocktail hour and I didn't want to miss it on my first night. So, now I'm just finishing my drink, the Maltese Falcon, which was made by the best bartender named Sam. He's truly fabulous," I praise. I hold my drink up as if toasting them before bringing the glass to my lips. "Mm," I murmur in appreciation as I take another sip of my drink. "And this drink is amazing! If you ever come to Malta, you absolutely have to order one," I emphasize. "Promise me," I prod, playfully.

"Oh!" I exclaim, my eyes wide, remembering. "You're never going to guess who I just saw inside, sitting right next to me at the bar," I prompt, shaking my head in disbelief. "No, it's not a big celebrity. I wish," I grumble, smirking. "It was none other than Mr. Personality himself," I announce, grimacing. Nodding my head in confirmation, I proclaim, "Yup, the guy in nine-C. He's staying at my resort. I'm not kidding," I reiterate. "But, I promise I'm not going to let him and his negativity ruin my vacation!" I reiterate.

"Miss, your table is ready," the same young man calls as he steps closer to the sitting area, interrupting my small tirade.

Looking up at him with a small, appreciative smile, I respond, "Thank you!" My table is ready a lot faster than I expected.

Turning my attention back to my phone, I inform my viewers, "Okay, I'm going to go and sit down at a table outside and enjoy the rest of my evening along with this drink." I hold up my glass towards my phone in another toast to my audience. "I promise I will take you guys exploring tomorrow. Maybe we'll go for a swim out by the pool before we go on an adventure," I suggest, still not quite sure what my plan will be. Giggling, I finish, "I guess you'll have to wait and see tomorrow! See you then! Ciao!" I tap to end the video and quickly upload it to my vlog as I stand, wondering if it will have any of the delays like the last one.

I make my way back to the outdoor podium, finding the gentleman who came to get me. He grins and prods, "Are you ready?"

"Yes, thank you," I respond, nodding my head in confirmation.

He escorts me to a table at the edge of the patio and pulls the chair out for me. "Is this okay, Miss?" he inquires, arching his eyebrows in question.

"This is perfect. Thank you," I repeat. I lower myself into the seat, the tables and chairs all an elegant wrought iron, with dark green cushions attached for comfort. I set my glass down in front of me and look around, happy to be by myself on the back patio of the restaurant. Smiling to myself, I can't help but feel content and extremely lucky to be here. Gazing out at my surroundings, I appreciate row after row of perfectly aligned grapevines, while anticipating the impending sunset over the horizon. I'm going to love having the vineyard on one side and the sea on the other. No matter where I go, I can't go wrong with the scenery. Every side of this resort seems to have an incredibly stunning view. I can only imagine what sightseeing will lead me to discover and I can't wait to find out. Picking up my glass, I take another sip of my drink and relax back into my seat.

The serenity in front of me seems to be helping me forget about nine-C. That man was so infuriating. It almost felt like he was trying to annoy me, but why would he do that? He doesn't even know me. I think he pushed me over the edge when he started challenging Sam. I wasn't about to let Sam get caught in the crossfire. He seems like much too kind of a man for that to happen. If nine-C keeps this up, I'm going to have to find a way to ask what his problem is without him getting even more irritated with me, but it seems inevitable that I'll keep running into him with both of us staying at the same resort. This place may be big, but it's not that big. How does a man that handsome have the audacity to be such a jerk to someone who's just trying to be nice to him? I truly don't understand. I grimace at my thoughts, wondering what his good looks have to do with anything. That's the last thing I should notice from a man who doesn't even show me common courtesy. I take another sip of my drink, noticing my glass is almost empty. I set it back down on the table, realizing nine-C has invaded my thoughts again. Is this supposed to be me forgetting about him? I grimace and attempt to push him out of my mind for what I promise myself will be the last time.

I glance around the patio, my eyes quickly sweeping over the people all around me, causing me to suddenly realize all of them are couples. Every single guest here seems to be either holding hands with someone, having what appears to be an intimate conversation with their faces close together or laughing together with pure love and adoration in their eyes. I grimace, reminded again that I am here alone. Even if this was never supposed to be a romantic vacation for me, seeing all these couples together, while I'm sitting here all by myself, and Kristen is back home with Barnaby, the sight causes my chest to tighten anyway. I quickly shake off my negativity, feeling as if nine-C's bad mood is starting to rub off on me, but I don't understand why. I usually don't let those kinds of things get to me. I'm happy with who I am and where I am in my life. I'm going to sit here, finish my drink and enjoy this spectacular view. I may never have another chance to be here relishing this and I'm not going to waste a moment of it feeling bad.

Sam steps up next to my table with a smile on his face and another cocktail in his hand. "For you, Miss," he offers. He sets a cocktail napkin down. Then, he carefully places the glass on the napkin, next to the empty one.

I feel my whole face light up and I return his kind smile as he straightens and looks down at me. "Thank you, Sam," I murmur, appreciatively.

"You are so very welcome. But, why are you all alone?" he inquiries, his eyes full of both curiosity and empathy.

I wince, his question almost mirroring my earlier thoughts. I take a deep breath and instantly attempt to brush it off. "Oh, it's a long story," I respond, waving my hand in front of me like it's no big deal. I do wish Kristen were here with me, but I'm determined to enjoy every part of this vacation without any regrets.

"No husband?" he probes.

"Oh, goodness, no," I retort.

"Boyfriend?" he prods.

I chuckle softly and shake my head in response. "Nope. I'm as single as they come," I proclaim. I sit up a little straighter, portraying my pride and confidence.

"But you come to a beautiful country. You should have someone to share it with," he claims.

Forcing a smile, I nod my head in agreement, as my thoughts again flicker to Kristen and all the time we spent planning and anticipating this trip. I may not have planned to share it with the love of my life, but I am disappointed I'm not able to share it with her. "My best friend Kristen was supposed to be here," I inform him.

"Ah," he murmurs.

"She's getting married in a month," I add.

"Ah," he brightens. "Congratulations! Is she in your hotel room?" he inquires.

Grimacing, I answer regretfully, "No, she had to cancel."

"You come to Malta by yourself?" he prods for clarification.

"Sure, why not?" I reply, shrugging my shoulders.

"Well," he begins, thinking about his explanation, "Malta is a very romantic country," he reiterates. The corners of his mouth tug upwards and I notice a sparkle in his eyes, just before he suggests, "Maybe you'll find a husband here."

I burst out laughing as I feel my face heat instantly. I can't help it. The only single person I've even seen since I arrived at the airport has probably been nine-C, my not so friendly seat neighbor. I catch my breath and look up at him from underneath my long eyelashes. Tilting my head to the side, I tease him, "Is that an offer Sam?"

He chuckles and looks away, as if embarrassed. He holds up his left hand, wiggling his fingers and showing off his simple gold wedding ring. "No!" he insists vehemently. "I'm married for seventeen years, now. We have four children," he adds, his chest puffing up with pride.

"That's lovely, Sam," I reply, sincerely.

"Thank you," he states, a smile lingering on his lips, his thoughts momentarily remaining on his family. Taking a deep breath and exhaling slowly, he pauses, glancing at me with slight hesitancy. Then, he takes another deep breath and I notice a sudden determination in his kind eyes. "I just don't want you to be alone," he emphasizes.

"I'm not alone, Sam. I have you, don't I?" I probe again, but this time he understands that I'm only teasing him.

He grins, shyly and emphasizes, "I mean for exploring some of the places we have to offer and having some fun outside of the hotel. It's true, Malta is safe for a single woman, but it's much too beautiful to keep to herself," he decrees.

I give him a reassuring smile, in attempt to let him know I'll be just fine on my own. "I'll take plenty of pictures," I state. I promised Kristen I would take pictures and share them with her when I get back. Plus, I want a lot of pictures to remember the trip by as well as some to share with my audience and maybe even a broader audience than before. I can surely hope.

He laughs in response and I quickly join in, giggling along with him. He nods his head in acknowledgement and finally relents, declaring, "Fair enough." He pauses, before asking, "Do you need anything else?"

I shake my head in answer. "No, thank you," I mumble. I pause for a moment, before I realize I never gave him my name. I am going to be here for two weeks and I couldn't ask for a kinder soul to talk to. "I'm Shea, by the way," I inform him, officially introducing myself as I hold out my hand.

His grin grows wider and he nods in acknowledgement as he accepts my hand. He lifts it to his lips, placing a kiss on the back of my hand in greeting. "Have a good evening, Miss Shea," he asserts, releasing my hand.

"You too Sam," I murmur as he picks up my empty glass. Then, he turns around and retreats back inside, politely greeting other guests as he passes by.

I smile to myself as I return my focus back to my first sunset in Malta, now almost completely disappearing behind the rows and rows of grapevines. The darkening night sky lights up in shades of yellow, orange, pink, and even some shades of purple, before the sun completely vanishes behind the horizon, turning day into night. The glow of the half-moon, the twinkling of the stars against a black backdrop, and small, white twinkle lights loosely strewn around the umbrellas of each table slowly replaces my view. The perfectly aligned rows of the grapevines remain the one constant, although now almost disappearing into the darkness.

Chapter 9

Shea

I wake up early with a smile on my face, even though I tossed and turned most of the night. I wanted to get some sleep before doing something today, but my body didn't agree. I'm not sure if it's because of my excitement from being on vacation or from the jetlag and time change, but either way I definitely didn't get enough sleep. There's no way I'm going to waste my day in my hotel room by attempting to sleep in, though. If I fall back asleep, I might miss the whole day. It seems I'm not going to get much sleep either way, so I might as well enjoy my time. Maybe going down to the pool will help me feel a little better.

Forcing myself to climb out of bed, I grab my navy blue one-piece bathing suit with a modest scoop neck and back and one-inch straps over my shoulders before striding into the bathroom to get ready. It doesn't take me long to cleanup, and get dressed. I reach for a hair tie and pull my hair up into a messy bun, before I glance in the mirror, satisfied. I step out of the bathroom, pulling a white net cover-up over my head. Then, I slip on my white flip-flops to wear down to the pool. I reach for my room key, phone and sunglasses, deciding that's all I'll need while I'm down there. I can get the rest after I come up to get ready for the day.

Making my way down to the pool, I grin at anyone I pass, which honestly isn't too many people with the sun barely up over the horizon. I step outside and follow the stone pathway back to the first pool. Looking around I notice I'm probably the only actual guest down here this early, but the sign does say the pool opens at sunrise. I see a few employees getting ready for guests as they begin to clean the area, wiping down the tables and chairs, as well as starting to open everything up for the day.

A tall, thin beautiful woman with olive skin and dark brown eyes saunters by me pushing a large green cart full of white beach towels, but she stops with a wide smile as she notices me. "Good morning, Miss," she begins. "Would you like a clean towel?" she offers.

"Sure, thank you," I murmur, appreciatively. Reaching out, I take the towel she holds out for me. "Have a good day!"

"Thank you and I hope you enjoy your day too!" she proclaims.

Walking over to one of the lounge chairs, I set my folded towel down on the end. I pull my cover-up over my head and double check my room key didn't fall out of the pocket before I toss it on the lounge chair. I set my sunglasses down on top of it before slipping out of my flip-flops. The smooth, cool stone instantly sends a small shiver up my spine, causing me to hesitate for just a moment. I know getting in the water will only make me colder, but hopefully it will also wake me up so I can enjoy the day seeing a little bit of Malta.

Clasping my phone in my right hand, I take a deep breath and stride for the edge of the pool. I momentarily lift my gaze, the view in front of me nearly taking my breath away. With the rocky edge and the gentle waves of the sea just beyond, I take a deep breath, assessing my current reality. I'm still having trouble believing I'm finally here. Strolling around the edge of the clear blue pool water, I make my way to the shallow end before I even dare stick my toes in, testing the water temperature. "It's not too bad," I mumble to myself. I grasp the silver railing and slowly descend down the steps into the shallow end of the pool. Tiptoeing a little further in, I stop when the water reaches just above my waist. Exhaling slowly, I try to relax, feeling my body release some of its built-up tension. Bouncing lightly on my toes in attempt to stay warm, I hold my phone above my head, deciding this is as good a time as any.

I open my phone and grin as I press record. "Good morning, Sheacationers," I proclaim, giggling at the made-up name. "I told you I was going to take a dip before going sightseeing today. It's a little before eight and let me tell you, this jetlag is so bad," I admit. "I honestly don't know what to do." Taking a deep breath in defeat, I request, "So if any of you have any suggestions, please leave it in the comments below or send me a DM (Direct Message). I will try anything at this point," I claim, pleading. I hope asking for assistance will help me figure out a way that will work for me to get myself back on track for this trip. "I think the nap I took yesterday really threw me off. I thought that getting in the pool this morning before I went sightseeing would wake me up, but the water is so perfect and warm," I croon my appreciation. "I'm even more relaxed now," I joke.

"For those of you who know me or have gotten to know me, you know that I don't know how to swim," I laugh humorlessly at the irony. "So, I'm sure you're surprised to see me in the water, but don't worry. I'm just hanging out here in the shallow end where I can stand. I promise I'm keeping myself safe."

I momentarily look around me in awe, just trying to come up with the simplest way to explain what I'm seeing, but it's not easy. "It's so beautiful here, guys," I murmur. "If Kristen were here, she would've slept in and then laid by the pool all day, enjoying the sunshine and the incredible view of the rocky shore and the water." I pause briefly at the thought of Kristen, but quickly push her out of my thoughts. "Well, now we get to do whatever we want!"

Standing up a little straighter, I continue, "Today, I'm going to start off by going to Crystal Lagoon. You can only get there by boat or hiking and of course I'm going to hike so I can take tons of pictures," I announce. "And don't worry," I add as an afterthought, "I'm going to take you with me the entire time."

Seeing movement out of the corner of my eye, I tear my gaze away from my phone and look around, noticing several guests milling about. "Oh," I mumble. "It looks like other guests are getting up and starting their day. So, I'm going to get out of the pool, grab some breakfast and head to Crystal Lagoon," I inform my viewers. "Make sure to follow my stories to check it out with me. Ciao!" I declare and blow a kiss to the camera before I tap to end the video. I tap to upload it as I carefully return to the pool steps and climb out of the water.

Making my way back to the lounge chair where I left my things, I grab the towel I laid there earlier and dry myself off the best I can, before dropping the towel and pulling my cover-up back on over my head, again verifying my room key still remains in the pocket. Checking to make sure the video uploaded to my vlog, I grin at the clear picture. I grab my sunglasses and slip them on as I slide into my flip-flops and begin meandering back to my room as I take in my surroundings.

It doesn't take me long to shower and get ready, the loud sound of my grumbling stomach causing me to speed up my normal routine. I glance in the mirror, taking in my reflection. I'm wearing faded cut-off jean shorts and a pale pink V-neck tank top, with strips of fabric crisscrossing between the V. I have my pink sneakers on, so I'll be comfortable and feel cute at the same time with my matching shoes. I pull my hair up into a high ponytail, wanting to keep it off my neck, since it looks like it will be warm and sunny today. I touch up my make-up, leaning closer to the mirror as I carefully apply my pink lip-gloss. I rub my lips together and break them apart with a soft pop. "I think I'm ready," I mumble to myself. I grab my black bag, with my camera safely tucked inside and toss my lip-gloss in before I sling it over my shoulder. I pick up my room key on the way out the door and slip it inside my bag right next to my phone and my wallet. I definitely don't want to forget that.

I make my way downstairs and walk into the resort's casual bar and restaurant, where they have a buffet set up every day for breakfast. I hand the greeter my room key and she quickly scans it, before looking back at me with a smile. "Go ahead and help yourself to the buffet," she offers, gesturing over her shoulder.

They have tables set up against the wall near the kitchen with all kinds of food, while juices and coffee appear to be set up on the bar. White tablecloths drape over the tables, covered with an enormous amount of food. I see all kinds of things, such as bagels, breads, muffins, donuts and pastries. Then there's bowls of all kinds of fresh fruit, both cut and whole pieces. I move down the line to find cereals, oatmeal, with more mix-in's than I think I've ever seen, yogurt, hard-boiled eggs and smoothies. Further down I find hot foods in stainless steel trays with a burner underneath to keep everything warm, including pancakes, French toast, scrambled eggs, bacon, sausage, hash browns mixed with vegetables like onions and peppers and even mini-omelets. I put some scrambled eggs and cut fruit on my plate, along with a banana muffin. Then I make my way to the bar and pour myself a glass of orange juice and a cup of coffee. I glance at everything and carefully prop the coffee cup on the edge of my plate, so I can attempt to carry everything at once.

I cautiously make my way to an empty table near the back doors, leading out to the patio. As I get closer to the vacant spot, I notice Nine-C, sitting and eating his breakfast right next to the only open space and press my lips tightly together. He has his back to me and he's dressed casually in a dark blue-gray t-shirt with a button at his neck, black shorts and black sneakers.

I set my food down at the table behind him, but he doesn't bother looking up to see who it is. I grimace and roll my eyes as I sit down on the stool with my back to his. I take a deep breath, reminding myself that I'm not going to let his negativity get to me. I'm going to keep being me, no matter how much he seems to push my buttons. I'm going to be nice to him, determined to enjoy my vacation. I put a smile on my face, hoping for a positive response, but definitely not expecting one. "Good morning, Nine-C," I greet him, cheerfully over my shoulder.

He looks up from his phone and barely spares me a glance from over his shoulder. He arches his eyebrows in surprise when his gaze lands on me. "Morning," he grumbles.

I flinch, annoyed with his reaction, but quickly control my features. He doesn't have to be so rude about it, every time he sees me. I take a sip of my orange juice and swallow it, but I just can't let this go anymore. It's driving me crazy. I'm on vacation and I don't deserve for him to be so rude when all I'm trying to do is be polite and show him some kindness. I glance over my shoulder and narrow my eyes at him. Then, I open my mouth and snap at him before I can think better of it. "You know, you could try being friendly."

"I could," he mutters, sarcastically, as he stares at his phone.

I clench my teeth and press my lips tightly together in irritation. I twist my body towards him, and inquire, "Did I do something to offend you?"

"No," he answers. He shakes his head and sets his phone down on the table, taking a drink of his orange juice.

I can't believe he doesn't even have the common courtesy to turn around and look at me. How can someone be so rude? "Well, it certainly seems like I did," I retort, not hiding my displeasure.

I turn back to my table and take a bite of fruit and a sip of my coffee. After a moment I hear him heave a sigh as he sets his glass down on the table. I don't know if it's from something that just happened or from me, but I really want to know. Call it curiosity, but I don't understand this man and for some reason I need to figure him out. "Look," he begins, startling me the moment I realize he's talking to me. I straighten slightly and turn my head towards him. I hold my breath, extremely curious to hear what he's about to reveal. "My brother was left at the altar and he asked me to go on his honeymoon with him," he explains.

I cringe, just imagining the pain his brother must be in. "Oh," I mumble. "Ouch," I concede, realizing there's a lot more to the handsome, but grumpy man from seat Nine-C than he's revealed to me. I should know better than to judge, but a person can only take so much negativity.

He grimaces and huffs a humorless laugh. Then, he nods his head in confirmation and enlightens me. "Yeah, and then he decided to leave me at the airport."

"Oh," I murmur as comprehension suddenly dawns on me. "That's the guy that gave me his ticket," I proclaim.

Abruptly, I realize how much the two of them look like brothers, now that I know the connection.

He nods his head in confirmation, "Yes. My brother, Daryl."

"Ah, I see," I mumble and take another bite of my eggs.

"I don't know why I didn't follow him," he grumbles, shaking his head in disappointment.

I grimace and turn to look at him, but he's still sitting with his back turned to me as he stares out the window appearing a little lost. A lump gets stuck in my throat, seeing his agony. He exhales a harsh breath and glances at his phone again before quickly pushing it away. He sighs and takes a sip of his orange juice. My heart clenches agonizingly, aching for his obvious pain. I feel the strongest urge to do everything I can to comfort this man, even though I'm not sure if he would even accept it, especially from me. I can't sit and do nothing though. I have to try. "Well, maybe you're supposed to be here," I suggest.

He huffs and shakes his head in disbelief, continuing to stare out the window, with a look in his eyes I can't quite decipher. "Yeah, maybe I'm supposed to spend Christmas all by myself the same year that my father died," he blurts out, sarcastically.

I gasp, feeling as if I were just punched in the chest with his overwhelming grief. "I'm so sorry," I whisper, hoping he hears the sincerity in my voice.

He sighs heavily and rasps under his breath, "Me too." I look over at him, not sure how to help him or even what to say. I wish I knew exactly what to do to make him feel better. "I shouldn't be here," he finally mutters, sounding defeated.

I close my eyes and take a deep breath, trying to gather my strength in hopes of alleviating some of his pain. I keep my body twisted towards him and attempt to encourage him to at least try to enjoy this trip. Maybe relaxing, exploring and just spending his time somewhere completely different than where he's from could be exactly what he needs. His brother obviously wanted him to still come on this trip, maybe his brother thought he needed it. "But you are," I softly emphasize. "There's no reason not to take advantage of it and do some sight-seeing," I propose.

He turns towards me a little bit, arching his eyebrows in surprise. "Alone?" he prompts. He shakes his head and grimaces. "No thanks," he mutters.

"Why not?" I question, arching my eyebrows in challenge. "I'm alone too. I'm going to the Crystal Lagoon today," I inform him. "You can come with me," I suggest, surprising myself as the words pass through my lips.

His eyes widen in shock, although I'm not sure if it's from the invitation or where I'm said I'm going. "You know there are all sorts of rock slides and stuff there, right?" he probes.

"Yeah," I concede, "but I still want to go and see how high it is in person. I want to climb it," I add, defiantly.

"Are you going to jump?" he questions.

I shake my head vehemently. "Oh, gosh, no! I don't know how to swim," I admit sheepishly. "I just want to take some pictures and enjoy the views.

He nods his head in acknowledgement. Then he mumbles, "Have fun," before he turns back to his breakfast and takes a bite of a roll.

My heart sinks into my stomach, as disappointment hits me hard with his response. I don't know what I expected after he's been so rude from the start, but it felt like he was starting to open up and I liked it. Plus, it sounds like he could use some company, whether he will admit it or not. "I take it you don't want to come?" I prod, hoping he might change his mind.

He shakes his head. "That's a hard pass," he answers firmly, making me flinch. Taking another bite of my breakfast, I decide not to push, when he takes me by surprise. "So what's your story?" he prompts. "Why are you here all by yourself?"

My heart skips a beat, at his sudden interest or maybe it's just curiosity, but it's definitely a good change of pace in my opinion. "I was left at the airport by my best friend," I admit, hesitant to turn around and see his reaction to my confession.

I feel him stop and stare at me with wide eyes, obviously taken aback. I peek at him over my shoulder, taking in his expression. "Some friend," he mumbles.

I shake my head, feeling the need to defend her. "It's not her fault. It was her fiancé, I guess," I concede and scrunch up my nose in displeasure. "He didn't want her gallivanting around the Mediterranean with a single girl," I reply, bitterly.

"Someone has trust issues," he mutters under his breath.

I chuckle softly. "Tell me about it," I concur. "I've known her since we were fifteen. Then, this guy comes into the picture and I can barely hang out with her anymore," I inform him.

"Tell her to run. Marriage isn't worth it, anyway," he advises.

My eyes widen in surprise at his comment. "Is that so?" I probe, curious as to why he's so cynical. I understand a little bit after what happened with his brother, but that doesn't explain his strong reaction to marriage.

He nods his head in confirmation and mumbles, "Yeah." He pauses, hesitating briefly, before he continues,

85

enlightening me with his explanation. "My brother's fiancé, well former fiancé," he corrects, "ran off with one of the groomsmen. His best friend from high school."

I wince and mumble, "Ouch! It sounds like it's a story right out of a movie."

He grimaces and nods his head in agreement. "Yeah," he murmurs.

"Well, it's not always like that," I attempt to tell him, although I don't think he'll really listen. It has to be hard when everything is still so fresh in your mind. Plus, seeing it happen to someone so close to you, someone he obviously cares about has to be even harder on your heart. I can't imagine watching someone I care about experience something like that.

"I wouldn't know. I've never been engaged," he states.

My stomach flip-flops at his comment, but I ignore it. "Me neither, but my parents have been married for thirty years," I announce.

"Mine would have been married for thirty-five," he comments, a reverent look on his face.

I gulp down the sudden lump in my throat and arch my eyebrows in challenge. "See? True love exists," I claim.

"For them maybe," he concedes. After a moment, he shakes his head and the corners of his mouth twitches up in amusement. He chuckles softly, lost in thought.

I can't help, but smile in response. "What's so funny?" I inquire.

"I'm sitting nearly halfway around the world, chatting with some stranger about true love," he states, letting me know how absurd he thinks this situation is, but I guess he's right.

I'm really enjoying talking to him, now that he's finally opening up to me. I see so much sadness in him and now I understand why he was so grumpy before. I don't want to push him to do something he doesn't want to do, but I do wish he would join me. But it's his decision either way. As for me, I need to enjoy this vacation I spent so much money on, even if I do that alone. I finish the last of my orange juice and set it down. Then I wipe my mouth with my napkin and leave it on the table as I stand up, ready to go exploring Malta. "Well, you could be with some stranger checking out the sights," I reiterate, trying one more time to encourage him to come along with me as he watches me thoughtfully. "See you later, Nine-C," I declare, grinning at him.

"Bye," he murmurs with a small smile on his face, making my heart clench again.

I grab my bag and glance at him one more time, before I turn and walk away. I step out the front door and find a tall, thin man, with tanned skin, brown hair and light toffee colored eyes wearing black pants and a tan button down shirt with a resort nametag pinned to his chest. He smiles and greets me, "Good morning, Miss. May I help you with anything this morning?" he inquires.

I nod my head, "Yes, could I please get a car to drive me to the area where I can climb up and overlook the Azure window?" I request, my excitement palpable.

He glances down at a piece of paper sitting atop his podium, before he nods his head, "Ah, yes." He looks up and steps over to the circular drive. He waves towards a white car parked along the side. "This driver will be happy to take you," he announces.

I grin and wave to the approaching car, my excitement returning. "Thank you," I tell him.

"Have fun!" he responds.

The sedan pulls up and I smile as I open the door and slip into the back seat before he has the chance to even unbuckle his seatbelt. "Hello," I say, cheerfully greeting the driver.

"Good morning, Miss," he acknowledges. "Where are we headed?" he asks.

"The Azure Window, please," I prompt.

He nods his head in acknowledgement and puts the car in drive. I stare out the window at the passing scenery as we go, trying to take everything in. It's not long before we pull off onto the side of the road. There's a stone wall about four feet tall following down the other side of the road, protecting the land. I look out, realizing we're near the shore. I step out of the car, seeing a few other tourists following a stone path to or from the path up the rock formation. I look back and reach into my purse, pulling out some money to pay the driver. "Grazzi," I say with a grateful smile.

"Ta' xejn," he replies, which I'll assume means you're welcome.

I close the door behind me as I take in the beauty of the cliffs and the water just beyond in various shades of blue. When I was looking into different places to see while visiting Malta, I found so many articles about the Azure window. The famous natural landmark was formed from a collapsed sea cave and stood as a natural rock arch, coming out of the water. It's been in so many movies and television shows over the years. Plus, people who enjoy cliff jumping have it on their must do lists, although I'm not one of them. Then, in 2017, it tragically collapsed into the sea during a terrible storm, devastating many. It's still an incredible view and it's still famous for jumping and diving, but I'll stick with observing.

I step off the road onto the dirt path, noticing a Warning sign, reading, "Danger, Unstable Cliffs. Stay Back." Well that's encouraging. I step onto the beach, stopping to look out at the water, appreciating its beauty.

I'm in awe of what remains of the Azure Window, now broken at the bridge at the top, with the water crashing down below. The colors of the rock include tans and grays as expected, but also oranges carved out by the sea and the weather Mother Nature has thrown its way. I notice small patches of green on top, but very minimal growth. I pull out my camera, snapping a few pictures, before spinning on my heel and beginning my trek up to the top.

Chapter 10

Michael

Watching her as she walks away, I grab my phone, continuing to look through my messages, most of them asking me how Daryl is holding up. I sigh and set my phone down on the table again. I finish my coffee and turn my head, glancing back at the chair she just vacated and wishing she were still here. A server steps up to the table and begins clearing the dirty dishes, instantly stopping my train of thought. I look at her and paste a smile on my face, hoping it doesn't make me look as crazy as I've been feeling the last few days. I stand up and trudge back to my room feeling defeated.

I step into my room and drop my key on the table as I walk in. Opening the sliding glass door, I wander out to the balcony. Taking a deep breath, I close my eyes, enjoying the heat of the sun. It's going to be a nice day. I can't help but think back to the beautiful woman on her way to see the sights of Malta. She should be able to see a lot today. I can't believe she invited me to go with her after how I've been to her. I smile to myself and gaze out at the view once again. Shaking my head in disbelief, I mumble out loud, "What am I still doing here?"

I swiftly turn back into my room, pick up my key and wallet and stalk out the door without wasting anymore time thinking about it or second-guessing myself. I stride to the front of the resort and step up to the man at the bellhop station. "Can I get a car?" I request.

Nodding his head in acknowledgment, he waves a car over, parked just outside the circle drive. "Here you are, Sir. Enjoy your day."

"Thank you," I acknowledge. I slide into the back and state my intentions. "The Azure Window, please." It doesn't take long before I'm on my way, hoping I'm right about where she started her day and I'm able to catch up to her.

We pull off to the side of the road near the shore. I quickly pay the driver and step out of the car. Glancing at my surroundings, I immediately notice people wandering down a dirt path and make my way over to the beach where it appears to begin. Stepping onto the small section of sand, I pause, unexpectedly hit with the overwhelming beauty right in front of me. I take it all in for just a moment before I turn towards the path. Jogging over the sand I quickly begin to climb over the rocks and rough terrain. Glancing up, my heart skips a beat at a streak of pale pink about halfway up the cliff. Smiling to myself, I quicken my pace, hoping it's really her.

As I near the top of the cliffs, I spot her almost immediately, feeling an overwhelming sense of relief, but I quickly push the thought away. She's standing close to the edge of the cliff where the arch begins, peering out at the view. It looks like she's holding something in her hands I can't quite decipher from back here. Slowly, I close the distance between us as I take in the scenery around her, the cliffs and water behind her and the boats anchored down below in a small cove, the edges of the land consistently jutting in and out. The clear, pale blue sky, along with the rest of the Earth's natural backdrop, seems to enhance her beauty, making it almost impossible for me to tear my gaze away from her. The thought brings a smile to my face without my consent and I swiftly shake off the thought. As I get closer, I finally realize she's fiddling with a camera, attempting to set it up on a tri-pod, but she appears a little bit frustrated and it seems to be increasing every second.

She looks up, as if she knows someone's watching her. Her eyes widen in surprise as they collide with mine, her mouth dropping slightly open at the sight of me. Then, almost instantly, her whole face lights up as she directs a broad smile at me, seemingly happy to see me here. "Nine-C! I didn't expect to see you here," she admits.

I offer her a crooked smile and shrug my shoulders in response. "Yeah, some girl told me that I should go sightseeing," I tease.

Her already bright smile grows and she jokes, "Smart girl."

I chuckle softly and mumble, "Maybe."

She giggles melodiously, the sound sending chills down my spine and my heart racing. Focusing on me, she encourages, "Come on, let me take a picture of you."

My eyes widen in surprise and I gesture to myself. "Me?" I prod. She nods her head in confirmation and I shake my head vehemently in response. "No," I declare, shaking my head, not sure why she would want my picture.

"Please?" she begs, sweetly. She purses her lips and scrunches up her nose adorably. Then she releases a breath and explains, "Okay, I'd really love for you to take a picture of me, but I need to set it up first. Please?" she repeats.

"Okay, okay," I concede. I feel like I can't say no to this girl. Maybe I just want to make up for my less than charming attitude at first. "Where do you want me to stand?" I inquire.

Her face lights up with my response. "Just get as close to the edge as you can," she instructs, like it isn't a big deal.

My heart drops into the pit of my stomach and my eyes go as wide as saucers. "Are you kidding?" I probe, my heart suddenly beating erratically. "I might fall."

She tilts her head to the side and simply asks, "Well, do you know how to swim?"

"Yeah, so?" I mumble and shrug my shoulders.

"So, what's the problem?" she prompts.

I grimace at her question, feeling my body heat in embarrassment. I sigh in defeat and finally confess, "I don't like heights."

"Okay," she acknowledges, with a small nod of her head in understanding. "Get a little close, then. However close is comfortable for you," she proposes.

I nod my head in agreement and cautiously wander a little closer to the edge. My stomach drops and then bounces up and down like I'm on a roller coaster when I'm about four feet away. "Is this okay?" I prod.

"It's fine," she claims, with a sweet smile.

Placing my hands on my hips, I look over at her and grin, waiting as she snaps a few pictures of me. The moment she pulls the camera away from her face, I take a few rapid steps away from the edge and closer to her. I breathe a sigh of relief and quickly attempt to cover it up. "I'll give you my email so you can send them to me," I suggest.

"Or you can buy them from my website," she murmurs, the corners of her mouth twitching up in amusement.

I gasp and my eyes widen in shock. "What?" I grumble, not expecting that from her. She's been so nice.

She bursts out laughing, not able to hold it in. Smirking, she insists, "I'm kidding! Come look," she encourages.

Chuckling, I shake my head in disbelief as I walk over to her. I reach out and hold one side of the camera, while she holds the other. As we stand shoulder to shoulder, I'm completely aware of her proximity, while she slowly flips through the images. I'm amazed at the vivid color and extreme clarity of the pictures. I can tell, just with a small glimpse, that these aren't normal photos from someone. This takes a lot of talent. "Wow," I mumble in awe. I glance at her out of the corner of my eye and praise, "These are really good."

Her cheeks instantly flush a beautiful shade of pink, but she smiles and swiftly graciously accepts the compliment. "Thanks." I watch as she gulps down the lump in her throat before she begins giving me directions. "All you have to do is look through here," she points to the viewfinder, "make sure it's in focus and then press this," she explains, pointing to a black button. "I already have all the settings in place, so if it doesn't go into focus, just turn this slowly until it does," she instructs, easily giving me a brief demonstration on how to turn the lens on the camera.

"Sounds easy enough," I acknowledge.

"Great. Thank you," she murmurs, appreciatively. She slips the strap from around her neck off and hands me the camera. Then, she walks over towards the edge of the cliff, with a slight bounce in her step. She's obviously happy, causing the corners of my mouth to tug upwards. She spins around and looks at me with a beautiful smile lighting up her whole face and making my chest clench.

Taking a deep breath and exhaling slowly, I attempt to focus on the task at hand. Holding the camera up to my face, I peer through the viewfinder and although I can see her, her image is anything but clear. "It's fuzzy," I inform her.

"Turn the focus around the lens a little," she directs.

I do as she says and grimace, her image appearing even blurrier with my adjustments. "I think I made it worse," I mutter.

She takes a step backwards and inquires, "Is that better?"

I look through the viewfinder again and play with the focus a little more like she showed me before I respond. "Not really," I answer honestly.

She takes another step back and prods, "How about this?"

"A little," I mumble, "but you're still kinda' fuzzy," I insist.

She takes another step back and sounding hopeful, she questions, "This?"

"Don't you have auto-focus on this thing?" I solicit, wanting to do a good job for her. I want her pictures to look at least halfway descent, especially since I saw the wonderful pictures she took of me. It's the least I can do after how I've been treating her.

She makes a funny sound as I look through the viewfinder, but now she's completely out of the frame. What did I do wrong? I shake my head, annoyed at myself. This shouldn't be that hard. "Now I can't see you at all," I tell her.

She doesn't answer me, so I lift my head. My breath catches in my throat and my heart instantly drops to my feet in fear, when the only thing I can see is the view. I swiftly scan the area around me, panicked, hoping she just stepped in a different direction, but she's nowhere to be found. I step closer to the edge of the cliff and glance over and down towards the water, barely able to breathe. My heart pounds hard against my ribcage, beating so rapidly, that all I hear is the flow of blood in my ears. I spot a small figure with brown hair down below in the water, with her arms flailing and thrashing wildly. She appears to be sinking fast. The memory of her flippant confession flashes through my mind like a neon sign. "She can't swim," I gasp, suddenly more terrified than I ever thought possible.

I quickly set her camera down and run as fast as I can off the edge of the cliff, without even thinking. I'm in the air for merely seconds, before I plunge into the water feet first, the warm salt water shocking as it engulfs me. Opening my eyes under water, I search all around me, but I don't see any sign of her. My lungs feel tight and I break the surface, gulping in a deep breath as I frantically look all around me, praying I find her. "Hey! Hey!" I call out, making me realize I still don't know her name. But there's no response. Taking another deep breath, I dive back down below the surface, desperately searching for her. I suddenly spot a blur of pink I think might be her, no longer even attempting to claw herself towards the surface. I use all my strength to swim towards her as fast as I can. I wrap my arm around her chest and under her arm with one hand and swim towards the surface with my free arm, kicking and pulling us with all the energy I can muster and praying she'll be okay.

We break the surface and I gasp for breath as I glance over at her, but she's unconscious. I quickly swim for the shore, pulling her along with me. The small waves attempt to control my direction, but I push harder, slicing through them with determination. As I approach the shore, I stand up, picking her up in the process and cradling her in my arms. The moment I'm out of the water I set her down gently onto the rocks. I roll her onto her side and firmly pat her on the back a few times with the heel of my hand, as if she's choking and hoping it works. She needs to be okay. She finally starts to cough and sputter, spitting out some seawater. Watching her, for the first time since she disappeared from my view, I feel like I'm able to catch my own breath. Exhaling in relief, I flop down next to her as reality sets in. She coughs a few more times, before she finally looks up at me, meeting my gaze. She's breathing heavily and her brown eyes are as wide as saucers. I don't think I've ever been more relieved or seen anything more beautiful in my entire life than I do right now.

"Are you okay?" I prompt.

She nods her head in response and coughs a few more times, attempting to clear all the water from her lungs. I can't believe that just happened. She stares at me in awe as I continue to try to wrap my head around the last few minutes. Just as it starts sinking in, she finally catches her breath and asks, "You jumped in after me?"

I shake my head and huff a humorless laugh at her question. "Yeah, of course I did," I state, a little puzzled by her surprise. Then again, I did just admit to her that I was afraid of heights.

We both sit quietly as we continue to catch our breath and calm our racing hearts. Then she glances at me and blurts out, "Did you get the picture?"

My eyes widen and my mouth drops open in shock. She almost drowns, I jump off a cliff to save her and she wants to know if I got the picture. "No," I laugh in response and she giggles along with me. I shake my head and answer, "No, no I did not get the picture."

She blushes a beautiful shade of pink and shrugs her shoulders as if she couldn't stop herself from asking. She laughs along with me as we both remain sitting in that spot, catching our breath and letting our heartbeats return to normal.

She looks down at her clothes and then looks at me and does the same. "I guess we should go back to the hotel and change," she suggests.

"We have to go back to the top first and hope your camera and all of our things are still there," I remind her.

She laughs and nods her head in agreement. "Oh, yeah."

Chapter 11

Shea

I step up to the front of the resort, with my bag, including my camera, slung over my shoulder and him right by my side. I'm grateful all of our things were still sitting on top of the cliff. I would've been really upset if something had happened to my camera, I concede. Then again, I'm just thankful I'm alive.

The moment I felt myself slip on the edge of the rocks, lose my balance and then fall over the edge, I froze. I felt too panicked to scream or even make a sound. Saying I felt petrified might be an understatement, but it wasn't the fall that scared me. Landing in the water and not knowing how to make it out absolutely terrified me. I don't think I've ever been so scared in my life. I didn't believe I could survive. I had an overpowering feeling of distress thinking about the reaction of my parents and Kristen if I didn't make it. Then, the last image I see in my mind takes me by surprise; his green eyes focusing on me as he smiles.

Then, I hit the water, the sensation shocking me to move. I remember thinking I have to try to push myself to the top, but what am I supposed to push on and which way do I go to get there? I felt completely turned around and panicked as the waves hit me over and over again. I gulped down mouthfuls of salt water, struggling to breathe. My lungs began to burn. I felt like I was spinning before I ran out of air and darkness began to overtake me. His arm suddenly wrapped around me pulling me to safety. I take a deep breath and shake my head, attempting to clear my fearful thoughts.

I glance over at him from underneath my long lashes, his wet clothes and shoes, weighing him down, just like mine. We're both still damp and the cushions inside my shoes squish and squeak with every single step I take, making walking extremely uncomfortable. I can't believe I fell into the water. I need to pay better attention to what I'm doing. I don't know what I would've done if he hadn't been there...

He reaches out and nudges my arm, interrupting my chilling thoughts and stopping me. "Are you sure you are okay?" he prompts as I turn towards him. I look up at him, my chest tightening at the concern I see in his eyes.

I offer him a comforting smile and nod my head. After what he just did for me, the last thing I want is for him to feel bad for me. I'm going to be fine, I tell myself. "Yeah. I really need to learn how to swim," I acknowledge.

"Or not fall off any cliffs," he teases, only half joking.

I feel my face heat and I huff a laugh. "Ha, yeah, that too," I concede, nodding my head. I stare at him, a little overwhelmed by how much my feelings have already changed for this man, just since this morning. In only a few hours he's gone from a handsome and frustrating man who I hope I never have to see again, to a man my heart goes out to for what he's going through and now this. He said he has a fear of heights and he didn't even hesitate to jump off a cliff today, for me. He saved my life and I'll be eternally grateful. My stomach kicks up the butterflies at the thought and I feel my face turn an even deeper shade of red.

He stares back at me, opening and closing his mouth as if he wants to say something, but he doesn't. Then he runs his hand through his damp, wavy hair and heaves a sigh, dropping his hands to his sides. He forces a tight smile and awkwardly stammers, "Okay, well, um, I ah, guess, have a good night."

"Yeah, you too," I reply, pasting my own smile on my face. A wave of disappointment hits me all at once, feeling like I stumbled and fell flat on my back. He turns and slowly starts retreating back towards his room, making my chest ache. I don't know how to explain it, but I know I don't want him to go. I want to spend more time with him, but with everything that happened with him before this, I'm not really sure what the right way is to approach it, but I'm not about to miss my chance. Before he gets too far, I gather my courage and finally call out, "Hey, Nine-C?"

He halts and spins back towards me, giving me a crooked smile. Maybe it's because of the nickname I keep calling him. "Yeah?" he prompts, curiously.

"Let me buy you dinner," I propose. Then, I bite my bottom lip, anxiously waiting for his response.

He smirks and strides back towards me, stopping right in front of me. He arches his eyebrows in challenge and questions, "You want to buy me dinner?"

I don't blame him for his reaction when I think about how he treated me up until just a few hours ago, but I know I don't want him to walk away. After everything he shared with me this morning at breakfast, I know he's not the man he portrayed himself to be before now. Tilting my head to the side, I look up at him from underneath my long lashes and gulp down the lump in my throat. "Well, yeah," I confirm. I shrug my shoulders and clasp my hand tightly around my bag, in attempt to keep myself from fidgeting. "It's the least I can do," I claim as if this might only be my way of saying thank you, but that's the furthest thing from the truth. "You saved my life," I remind him as if I'm giving him new information. The simple fact causes my whole body to turn a deep shade of red. I take a deep breath and exhale slowly to help calm my anxiety.

The corners of his mouth twitch up in amusement. "Well, when you put it that way," he murmurs, trailing off.

We both laugh in response, helping me rid myself of my nerves. "Down here in an hour?" I suggest.

His green eyes sparkle as he grins and nods his head in agreement. "Yeah, sure," he murmurs softly.

"Okay. Great," I acknowledge, exhaling in relief. I look up at him, not able to wipe the smile off my face. I can admit to myself I'm thrilled he's taking me up on my offer. It's almost unbelievable how much my viewpoint has changed in such a short time, but extreme circumstances tend to change things in an instant.

"Can I walk you to your room?" he requests. He clasps his hands behind his back and rocks back and forth on his heels, waiting for my answer.

My heart skips a beat at his offer, but I need to decline at the moment. I shake my head and regretfully mumble, "No, thanks." Glancing at him, I admit, "I'm going to grab a cup of tea before I go up. My nerves are still shot."

He gives me a reassuring smile and nods his head in understanding. "I think I'll have something a little stronger at dinner," he reveals.

I laugh in response and swiftly agree, "Yeah, same." I stand in front of him, staring and wanting to say so much more to him, but I'm honestly not even sure what. It's like I'm looking for a reason to continue talking to him, but I will have that chance later tonight. After all, he did agree to have dinner with me, I remind myself.

"Okay," he begins. "So, an hour," he reiterates.

I nod my head in confirmation. "Yep, an hour." It won't take me that long to get ready. Plus, I don't think I'll be able to wait longer than that to see him again.

"Okay, see you then," he mumbles. Then he turns on his heel once again to head back to his room.

Watching him, I hesitate for just a moment before I stop him, calling out to him one more time, "Hey, Nine-C!"

He chuckles and shakes his head in amusement. He stops and turns around to face me again, finding me grinning broadly at him. "Yeah?" he prods.

"You got a name?" I inquire playfully.

He smirks and nods his head in acknowledgement. "Yeah, I do," he confirms. Then he gives me a mischievous grin, before he turns and strides away, this time not looking back.

I laugh as I watch him go until he disappears around the corner. Then, I turn around and saunter into the restaurant to get myself a cup of tea and bring it back to my room with me, hoping it will help calm my nerves. I'm ready to get these wet clothes off and get myself cleaned up, especially these shoes. I don't think these will ever dry.

Smiling politely, I order a cup of tea and step into the back corner to wait. With a few quiet minutes, I pull out my phone and hold it out in front of me ready to record another vlog. I tap record and begin, "Hi, guys! You're probably wondering why I look like a drowned rat, especially since you saw me in a bathing suit this morning. As some of you already know, the truth is I don't know how to swim," I concede self-consciously. I never learned and in the pool this morning, I was able to touch the ground and just walk, but later today it was a completely different story. You will never guess how it ends," I add, shaking my head in disbelief.

"So, I went to the Crystal Lagoon and I was standing on the cliff taking pictures. The views there are absolutely spectacular. Anyway, our buddy, Nine-C, shows up. I had asked him to go sight-seeing with me to be nice, but I never thought he would actually just show up after he turned me down." Shaking my head in surprise, I inform them, "Well, he did."

"So, to make a long story short, I was standing on the cliff while he was trying to take my picture for me and I fell off the cliff into the Mediterranean Sea." I heave a humorless laugh, my eyes wide with fear at the recent memory. "I don't even know how deep it was. Well, the next thing I know is he was in the water and he saved me. I swallowed a ton of salt water. I blacked out here and there, but he saved me," I murmur, still a little bit in shock. "I don't even know his name," I reiterate, in amusement. "He doesn't even know my name and he jumped in after me and he saved my life." I laugh at the irony. "Can you believe it? It's like the beginning of a weird fairy tale," I grin, his smile again on my mind. "Maybe," I add, reverently. "Anyway, I invited him to dinner later, so I will report back and let you know his name," I giggle.

"And yeah, I'm totally fine. I promise," I emphasize. "I'm just back at the hotel. I ordered a cup of tea to calm my nerves from the fall and my impending date with Nine-C." I smile to myself and concede, "Maybe he's not the jerk I thought he was." Pausing, I add, "Maybe!" I laugh and finish the vlog, "Okay. Ciao for now!" I blow a kiss at the camera and tap to end the video. I upload the video and slip my phone back into my purse.

"Your tea is ready, Miss," the barista politely informs me.

Stepping back up to the counter, I carefully reach for the cup of tea and smile, "Thank you," I tell her gratefully. I take a sip before I turn and stride back outside, taking my time as I saunter back to my room.

I open my door and set my bag down on the floor as I drop the key on the top of the dresser near the television. I kick off my shoes and breathe a sigh of relief as my feet step onto the smooth tile floor, without the squish between my toes. I lift the cup to my lips and take a small sip as the seriousness of what just happened practically overwhelms me. I walk over and sit down on the edge of the bed. What was I thinking? If it wasn't for him...I shake my head, ridding myself of the depressing thought. Stop saying what if. He *was* there and he jumped in to save me without even thinking twice. Knowing he has a fear of heights just makes what happened more impactful. He's my real life hero. I put my free hand over my chest, momentarily overcome with emotions. Taking a deep breath, I exhale slowly, trying to pull myself together.

After a few minutes, I start feeling a little better. I stand and walk over to my bag and pull my phone out. Turning it on, I pull up Kristen's contact. I begin typing, wanting to tell her what happened, but I don't want her to worry about me either. I bite my lower lip, thinking. Finally, I erase what I wrote and settle on telling her about Nine-C. "I have a date tonight," I type out and press send before I have a chance to second-guess myself.

Before I even have the chance to set my phone down, the bubbles begin dancing across the screen of our text window, letting me know she's already responding. "What? I want all the details!" she demands.

I giggle, knowing she'll be shocked reading my next words. "The guy from the plane," is my only response. If I tell her I don't know his name without telling her the whole story, I'll get a lecture instead of encouragement.

She immediately sends several surprised emojis back to me. Then, my phone beeps again with another message asking, "How did that happen?"

I pause, looking for a simple answer, when there really isn't one. "We ran into each other at breakfast and then again at the Azure Window. He's not at all what I thought. He just had a tough year," I reply, not wanting to give her details, yet.

"I want to know more!" she exclaims.

I laugh and quickly type out, "I have to go get ready."

She sends me a sad face emoji, before she concedes. "Okay. I guess I can wait until we chat. I expect to hear from you soon!" she insists. "Go get ready for your date and we'll talk later!" she encourages.

"Thanks," I tell her.

"Have fun!" she adds.

I smile and drop my phone down on the bed, as I finish my tea. Leaving the cup on the desk, I jump in the shower, quickly cleaning up. As I step out of the shower, I slip on the lush white resort robe as I do my make up. I pull my camera out of my bag and turn it on, skimming through the last few pictures of him standing at the Azure window. Butterflies instantly take flight in my stomach and my whole body warms as the corners of my mouth tug upwards. Looking away from the pictures, I glance out at the balcony, again noticing the incredible view. I haven't taken any pictures out there yet. I might as well take a few now before I forget. Making my way over to the sliding glass door, I pull it open. I step outside onto the balcony and lean against the rail, as I lift my camera to my face and begin taking pictures. I know I need to get ready, but taking pictures always helps to calm me down.

Just as I'm feeling myself finally relax and ready to go inside to figure out what I'm going to wear, I spot one more angle I have to take with my camera. I hold it up to my face and snap another picture. The camera clicks softly just as I hear the deep rumble of his voice, talking to someone. My heart jumps up to my throat as he steps out onto the balcony right next to mine, already showered. He has his phone pressed to his ear and he's dressed in navy blue dress pants and a pale blue button down shirt, not yet buttoned, his tanned, firm skin peeking through. "The girl you gave your ticket to," he states, chuckling. I freeze and attempt to gulp down the lump in my throat, realizing he's talking about me. He leans on the railing as he speaks, and my heart pounds so hard, I can barely hear his words over the rush of blood in my ears. Then, after a couple minutes, he finally turns and glances in my direction, startling as he meets my surprised gaze. I feel myself blush as I smile back at him.

Chapter 12

Michael

I sigh and run my free hand through my wavy wet hair, with my other hand clasping my phone. I can hear it in Daryl's voice that he doesn't want to talk about her anymore. I don't blame him, so I quickly change the subject. "So, how's mom doing?" I inquire.

"She's fine," he replies. "She was pretty upset when I walked in without you," he reluctantly concedes.

I laugh humorlessly knowing how she feels and grumble, "I can imagine." I shake my head in disbelief even though he can't see me. "I was pretty upset when you left me at the airport," I emphasize, reiterating the fact. I want to remind him how he was the one who pressured me to go on this trip without him. I don't want mom to be upset with me. I honestly don't want to see her hurting at all anymore. She's been through enough.

He sighs heavily and apologizes again. "I'm sorry, Mikey. I just couldn't go through with the honeymoon for a wedding that never happened," he grumbles. I know that's only part of his truth, but I'm not going to call him on it right now. He doesn't need that from me.

"I get it. Seriously," I emphasize, attempting to portray my sincerity. He has enough to worry about without adding me to the mix. "And honestly, I could have decided not to get on the plane and gone home with you," I remind him, attempting to take away his self-blame.

"I wouldn't have let you," he proclaims. "I felt like I needed someone to go on this vacation. Nearly fifteen grand and I didn't get insurance," he states, with clear aggravation in his voice. "You did me a favor," he reiterates.

I don't know if I buy his explanation, but for his sake I let him run with it. "I guess," I mumble in response.

"I just feel bad that you're going to be alone on Christmas," he acknowledges.

My heart skips a beat and I step away from the vanity mirror and step over to the sliding glass door and pull it open, stepping outside onto the balcony for some fresh air. "Actually," I begin, taking a deep breath. I'm a little hesitant to say anything, but he's my brother. "I don't think I'm going to be alone for Christmas," I finally blurt out, what I hope might end up being the truth.

"You're kidding," Daryl mumbles, the shock in his voice evident. "You met someone?" he prompts.

A smile tugs at my lips as I think about her. "Yeah," I admit. "The girl you gave your ticket to," I inform him, smirking.

"No way!" he exclaims.

I chuckle softly and shake my head, a little astonished about the whole thing myself. "I know," I mumble. "It's crazy. We're staying in the same hotel," I inform him. "I kind of had breakfast with her," I add tentatively.

"Kind of?" he questions, confused.

I lean on the railing looking out at the view, smiling at the memory. "Well, technically she sat at the table next to me, but she talked to me the whole time," I explain. We both laugh at my comment. "But we are having dinner together tonight," I declare.

"Come on. Seriously?" he probes, sounding surprised.

I nod my head even though he can't see me. "Seriously," I confirm.

"How did you ask her?" he pushes. Then he clarifies, "I mean, you've only been there for one day and I know you don't work fast with women."

"Ha, ha, ha," I grumble, even though I know he's right. He laughs at my reaction and I wait for him to quiet before I elaborate. "She actually asked me to dinner," I reveal.

He huffs another laugh and announces, "That sounds more like it."

"Shut up," I mutter, playfully, knowing he's just giving me a hard time. "She wants to thank me for helping her," I tell him.

"Helping her?" he repeats. "What did you do?" he prompts.

"You wouldn't believe me if I told you," I claim. I shake my head, still struggling to believe it myself.

"Try me," he insists.

"She fell off a cliff into the Mediterranean Sea and I jumped in and saved her," I enlighten him, knowing it will be hard for him to imagine.

I don't hear anything, but silence momentarily. Then, he suddenly bursts out laughing. I heave a sigh and wait for him to calm down. "You really had me going there, Mikey," he proclaims, still laughing at my expense.

"I'm serious," I state defensively.

"I call BS," he proclaims. "What's her name?" he questions, trying to catch me in the lie, but it's the truth.

"It's not BS," I insist, knowing I still can't answer the other part of his question. I can't believe I still don't know her name.

"How high up were you?" he demands.

"I have no idea," I reply, exasperated. "I don't want to even think about it," I emphasize, feeling my anxiety increase every time I do. A shudder runs through me and I take a deep breath, exhaling slowly before I continue.

"We were on top of the Azure Window," I add, hoping that will give him an idea.

I hear him stutter before he speaks. "Mikey, that's like a hundred feet up. You could have been killed," he tells me accusingly, what we both already know.

"It's like fifty," I correct, "but I didn't think about that," I insist. "She fell off and I knew she couldn't swim," I reveal. I didn't have any other choice. I would do it again in a heartbeat.

"You risked your life for this girl?" he pushes.

"I didn't think of it that way. I just..." I pause and gulp down the sudden lump in my throat. "I didn't want anything to happen to her," I murmur. I take a deep breath and admit, "She's really special, Daryl. There's just something about her."

"There must be," he mutters

"I can't explain it. There's this connection that I've just never felt before. I mean, she's smart, funny and beautiful. She's got this spirit that I just can't help but want to be around," I say in attempt to describe what I'm thinking. "You know?" I prompt.

"Well, you risked your life for this girl, so there must be something," he repeats. He sighs and questions again, "What's her name?"

I wince and push off the railing. I was hoping he wouldn't repeat that question. I don't want to explain the whole story, so I just answer honestly. "I don't know her name," I murmur.

"You don't know her name?" he prods, with clear disbelief.

I huff a laugh and confirm, "No, I don't know her name." Then I add, "I was planning on asking her at dinner tonight."

He laughs at my answer. "You better," he insists, clearly amused. "Especially if you're going to spend

Christmas with her." I turn and my eyes land on the subject of our conversation. She's standing on the balcony right next to mine wrapped in a plush resort robe with a camera in her hand, while she stares at me with a smile on her face. I smile back, instantly taken in by her beauty causing my stomach to twist. I gape at her, feeling my own face heat almost instantly. How much of my conversation did she just hear? My throat goes dry and then I decide it doesn't matter. Whatever she heard, I'm okay with it. I give her a tentative smile and she grins broadly, helping me relax.

"Hello! Mikey," I hear my brother prod from the other end of the line, pulling me back into our conversation.

"Yeah, yeah," I stammer. "I'm here. I gotta' go," I blurt out. I may be okay with what she heard, but I'm not okay continuing to have this conversation while I know she's watching me.

"Everything okay?" he questions, sounding confused by my sudden change in demeanor and urgency to get off the phone.

"Yeah," I confirm. "Love you. Tell mom and Ang I miss them," I request.

"All right," he quickly agrees. "Love you too, Bro," he mumbles. "Try to have some fun," he pushes.

"I will," I concur, while my eyes remain lingering on her. "Bye," I say. Then, I click end, before he has the chance to say anything else. I slip my phone into my pocket and take a step closer to the wall dividing our two balconies.

I watch her as she puts her camera down on a small round table, sitting between the two white patio chairs. Then she steps all the way up to the wall and reaches over the top, holding her hand out towards me. "Shea," she proclaims, grinning.

112

My eyebrows draw down in confusion and I prod, "Excuse me?"

"Shea," she repeats. "Shea Andrews," she adds with a bright smile.

I grin back at her as I take her hand in mine. I gasp, feeling a zap shoot up my arm the moment her soft skin comes into contact with mine. I quickly clear my throat and introduce myself. "Michael Foster."

"Nice to meet you," she replies.

She pulls her hand back and I reluctantly release it, smiling at her. "It's nice to meet you too," I state.

"If you'll excuse me," she murmurs, "I need to go get ready for my date." My grin widens and my chest tightens in response. Then, I watch as she spins towards the sliding glass door and pulls it open. She pauses and glances back at me. "I'll see you in ten minutes," she declares.

I arch my eyebrows in challenge. I'll believe that when I see it. She steps inside and closes the door behind her, followed by her curtains. I chuckle to myself as I smile at the closed door. Then, I turn and step back inside my own sliding glass door and close it behind me.

I stride back towards the bathroom to finish getting ready. I button up my shirt and tuck it in. I touch up my hair and smile to myself as I take one last look in the mirror. "Shea," I mumble to myself. I like that.

I pull my phone out of my pocket and text my brother. "Her name is Shea," I answer his earlier question. I slip my phone back in my pocket, ignoring the alert as it comes through, notifying me of a text message. He can wait.

I grab my room key and my wallet and slip them into my pocket, before I make my way downstairs to meet Shea. I know I'll arrive before her, but I want this to go well. I take my time strolling over to the restaurant. The hostess greets me as I approach, "Good evening. Are you a guest or are you just dining with us tonight?" She's wearing a sleeveless V-neck black dress with a resort nametag pinned to her dress adorned with her name on it. She has brown hair pinned up in a tight bun at the back of her neck, brown eyes and a polite smile.

"Um, I'm a guest, Michael Foster, but I'm waiting for someone, another guest, Shea Andrews. She should be here soon," I stammer, awkwardly.

She grins and nods in acknowledgement. "Would you like to sit down while you wait?" she offers.

I shake my head and reply, "No, thank you."

After a few minutes of me pacing while she stares at me, she prompts, "Are you sure you don't want to sit yet, Mr. Foster?"

I pause my pacing and stop to look at her. I shake my head again and insist, "No, it's okay. She should be here any minute," I reiterate.

The hostess glances over my shoulder and smiles. She nods in the direction she's looking and inquires, "Is that her?"

If it is her, I'm impressed she's only a few minutes late. She was still wrapped up in a robe a few minutes ago. She's not like most girls, but that doesn't surprise me if she can put up with me when I'm miserable and rude. I turn around and my breath catches in my throat at the sight of Shea descending the stairs into the restaurant, looking absolutely stunning. She's wearing a gorgeous red dress with three-quarter length sleeves. It almost appears as if the material is wrapped around her, crossing at a V just below her neck and gathering on her left side, causing it to sweep down the front in layers. She has the dress paired with strappy, black high-heeled shoes, bringing her a couple inches closer to my height. She's wearing her hair down again, parted on the left and brushed towards the right, looking silky smooth.

She smiles brightly as she approaches me, lighting up the whole room and causing my heart to skip a beat. I return her smile, truly grateful that I'm here. No, she's not at all like most girls, she's special. I want to know every little thing about her.

Chapter 13

Shea

I hang onto the rail as I descend the stairs, careful of every step. One big fall is enough for a lifetime, let alone for one day. I stop in front of Michael and smile up at him. "Nine-C," I greet him, playfully. "Don't you clean up nicely?"

"You're not so bad yourself," he replies, with a mischievous sparkle in his mesmerizing green eyes and the corners of his lips curving up in a grin.

"Shall I show you to your table?" the hostess offers, interrupting us.

Tearing our gazes from each other, we both turn our attention to her. Michael nods his head in acknowledgment. "Yes, please," he agrees.

"Follow me," she states.

He takes a step back and holds his hand out for me to go in front of him. "After you," he proclaims.

"Thank you," I acknowledge, not able to wipe the smile from my face.

I follow the hostess, distinctly aware that Michael is following right behind me, making my heart race. We step into a small room with windows on three sides overlooking the vineyard and a beautiful stone fireplace as the room's centerpiece, the flames flickering brightly inside. As we reach the table, he steps up beside me and pulls out my seat for me. I smile up at him and murmur, "Thank you," before I slip into the seat. He assists me in scooting me in.

Striding around the table, he sits down across from me as the hostess hands us our menus. Our waitress soon follows her, wearing black pants and a short sleeve black button down shirt, with the resort nametag pinned to her chest and her brown hair pulled back into a tight bun at the back of her neck. "Would you like something to drink?" she inquires.

"Do you like wine?" I ask, glancing at Michael.

He nods his head and replies, "I do."

"May I suggest a glass of our pinot noir?" the waitress recommends.

"That sounds perfect," I concur, as Michael nods his head in agreement.

"I'll be right back," she murmurs and turns around, walking away.

She returns quickly with our drinks and takes our order, before retreating back to the kitchen. I look up at him from underneath my eyelashes, realizing we finally have the chance to talk. My nerves quickly dissipate as we easily fall into a good conversation with both comfortable and playful banter. We begin sharing stories and soon I forget about all the other couples around us. It's almost like we're the only two in the room. I'm not able to wipe the smile from my face.

"It was awful!" he proclaims. "The entire car of people were staring at me as I walked face-first into the garage door," he concludes.

My head falls back as I burst out laughing, picturing it. "How embarrassing!" I exclaim.

"Told you I could top yours," he taunts, chuckling. "Okay, your best Christmas ever," he prompts.

"Ooh, that's a tough one," I mumble, pausing to think. "Christmas is always so big in my family," I say, explaining my hesitation.

His eyebrows draw down in confusion. "Then what are you doing here? How come you're not at home?" he questions.

I grimace at the reminder. "Like I said, Kristen and I had been planning this trip since like the day after she got engaged," I reiterate.

"How long ago was that?" he probes.

"Eighteen months," I answer.

His eyes widen in surprise. "And she cancelled, just like that?" he probes.

I press my lips tightly together and nod my head in affirmation. "Just like that," I mutter, still slightly frustrated at the memory.

"So why didn't you just stay home?" he prods.

"This trip took half of my life savings. I even worked two extra jobs to pay for it to be totally over the top," I enlighten him. "I wasn't about to walk away from that, even if Barnaby offered to pay me back," I explain, bitterly.

He smirks and clarifies, "Barnaby?"

My whole body tenses at just the thought of that man, but then I chuckle at Michael's reaction to his name. "Kristen's jerk fiancé," I grit out through my teeth.

"Anyone with a name like that sounds like he would be a jerk," he proclaims, chuckling and bringing an even broader smile to my face.

"He's a stockbroker," I inform him and he throws his hands up as if that's the cherry on top. "He really looks down his nose at me. Says I don't have a job, but a hobby instead," I reveal. I can't help, but feel resentful towards him. I have my doubts about how he truly feels about Kristen too, but she's in love with him.

"Well, what do you do for a job, anyway?" he inquires, changing the subject.

"I'm a photographer," I reply, my smile returning to my face.

"Really?" he questions, his eyes lighting up with curiosity.

I nod my head in confirmation, "Yeah. Mostly weddings and some private schools, but it pays the bills and I own my own business, so I can take time off for things like this," I elaborate. "How about you?" I prompt.

"I'm an editor for an online magazine," he reveals.

"No kidding! I've started doing some photojournalism," I tell him, excited to share this kind of connection.

"Really?" he asks, arching his eyebrow in curiosity. "I'm the sports editor for Fire Magazine online," he informs me.

My mouth drops open in surprise. "Shut up!" I exclaim. "They just used some of my photos for a story on East Coast Wineries," I apprise him.

"Nick Housey wrote that article," he comments.

I nod my head in confirmation, "Yes! I went to college with Nick."

He huffs a laugh and shakes his head in disbelief. "This is getting weird," he mumbles. "Nick and I grew up together," he enlightens me.

My eyes widen in surprise. "Ooh, I'll have to get all of the details about you from him," I taunt, the corners of my mouth twitching up in amusement.

"Or you can always find them out yourself," he suggests, bringing a huge smile to my face.

I feel my face heat again, so I clear my throat and change the subject, attempting to get the focus off of me. "So, what about you? What's your best Christmas ever?" I prompt.

He pauses, a small smile playing on his lips. "Come to think of it, this one might be up in my top three," he admits.

My face heats, turning an even deeper shade of red as butterflies twist and twirl in my stomach. My heartbeat picks up its pace and I stare into his eyes, not able to look away from his gaze. A man with a short-sleeved pale blue dress shirt, with a tan and mahogany acoustic guitar slung over his shoulder and hanging in front of his body, pulls our attention to him as he approaches our table. He's about five feet six inches with brown hair and eyes, tanned skin and a friendly smile. He nods at me and smiles and then turns to Michael with the same smile. "A very good evening to you," he carefully articulates. "If you tell me your wedding song, I will play it for your bride," he proposes.

Michael's eyebrows draw down in confusion and he chuckles softly. "My bride?" he prods.

I bite my lower lip, attempting to hold in my laughter, but it almost immediately escapes, bubbling out of me. I shake my head in gentle denial. "We're not married," I broadcast.

He nods his head in understanding and gives us a knowing grin. "Not yet, eh? Perhaps for your fiancé then?" he prompts.

Holding my hand over my mouth to muffle my laughter, I watch momentarily as Michael fidgets, awkwardly, his cheeks tingeing a light pink. Then, I jump in, holding my left hand up to see. I wiggle my fingers and playfully joke, "He hasn't proposed, yet." Michael chuckles softly, appearing slightly relieved by my reaction as he shakes his head in amusement.

"Why not?" he questions. "You are clearly so very in love," he observes, grinning.

Michael arches his eyebrows in surprise. "Are we?" he challenges, the corners of his lips curving upwards.

"Anyone can see," he states, confidently. "You're meant for each other. Tell me your song and I play so you can dance with your lady," he offers.

"We don't have a song," he murmurs. "Well, not yet, at least."

"Oh, should we have a song?" I ask, lightheartedly.

"Of course we should," Michael claims, bringing another smile to my face.

"Perhaps I should play one for you," the man suggests.

"An original song?" Michael questions.

"Yes, just for you," he reiterates.

"Just for us?" I repeat. "Really?"

Of course, I see that your love is something special. You should have a special song for it," the guitarist emphasizes.

"Okay, here's the deal," Michael begins. "If you play us an original song, I will get up and dance with her right here and now." He grins as he glances at me.

"Oh, really?" I ask, arching my eyebrow.

He winks, causing my heart to skip a beat. "And I'll give you twenty Euros," he offers.

"Okay," the guitarist happily agrees and nods his head. "Give me one moment," he requests, as he begins to strum his guitar.

"You can't be serious," I mumble shaking my head in disbelief.

"What?" he questions.

"Michael, come on," I urge, surprised he's pushing this.

"You don't want to dance with me, Shea?" he challenges.

"I never said that," I emphasize.

"He's never going to be able to come up with an original song that fast and play it for us. I guarantee it will be something we've heard before," he claims with a confidence I don't quite believe.

At that moment, the man begins singing along with his strumming, "On my way back home." Our eyebrows draw down in confusion, not recognizing the tune or the lyrics as he continues, "With the scent of you on my clothes."

Michael's mouth drops open in shock as he points to him impressed, making me laugh. He thought he had him, but this guy seems pretty talented. I watch as Michael shrugs and pulls twenty Euros from his wallet, shaking his head in disbelief. He stands and slips it in the guitarist's pocket at his chest. The man smiles in appreciation at Michael, instantly focusing back on his music. Then, Michael walks over to me and holds his hand out, arching his eyebrow in question. "A deal is a deal," he proclaims.

"That was your deal, not mine," I smirk.

The guitarist continues, singing, "Tonight the roads don't seem so lonely, when I have you."

"Well, apparently you're my girl. You're not going to leave me high and dry, are you?" he pushes, the corners of his mouth twitching up in amusement.

I laugh and grasp Michael's hand, as I stand up from my seat. He keeps hold of my hand as he rests his other one at my waist, my skin burning at his light touch. Reaching up, I place my free hand on his shoulders, near his neck, while we start to glide back and forth in time to the music. "I feel like I'm in an old time movie," I confess as the guitarist's silky voice fades into the background and Michael is the only one I hear or see.

He smirks and nods his head in acknowledgement. Then he shrugs his shoulders and replies, "Well, we do have a bartender named Sam."

"Touche," I respond, grinning wide.

"'The Maltese Falcon' and 'Casablanca,'" he murmurs, shaking his head with a subtle grin. "I feel like people don't know the difference anymore."

"I do," I claim.

He smiles proudly down at me. "I noticed," he states, making me blush. "You're going to get me into some sort of trouble, aren't you?"

A line from one of the movies instantly pops into my head and I fight my smile as I slip my hand from his sliding my other hand around his neck, his hand falling lightly to my waist. Then, I repeat the line out loud, attempting to appear nonchalant. "I don't mind a reasonable amount of trouble."

He chuckles softly and I smile up at him, my heart racing. He glances down at my lips and then my eyes, as if asking permission before he tilts his head towards me. I think I stop breathing as I tilt my head up towards him, my stomach twisting into knots in anticipation. He slowly begins to close the distance between us. My lips part just a little bit, ready for him to kiss me. I nearly stop breathing when he's close enough that I feel his warm breath on my face.

"Excuse me?" the waitress interrupts with her thick accent, instantly bringing us both back to reality. We both drop our hands to our sides and take a step back from one another, startled. "Your dinner is served," she announces.

I paste a smile on my face and mumble, "Thank you." Then, I quickly slip back into my seat as Michael does the same. She walks away and we break into laughter, as if we were just caught getting into trouble.

Chapter 14

Michael

After dinner, I sit with Shea, continuing to get to know her and laughing more than I recall doing in quite a long time. I honestly don't remember the last time I had this much fun just talking and spending time with anyone. I can't stop smiling. She keeps surprising me, moment to moment and she's already pushing me to be a better version of myself without even realizing it. Plus, she has the guts to call me out when I'm being unreasonable. I don't want this night to end.

Earlier, just knowing that Christmas is only a few days away and I'll be here without my family caused me a lot of stress. I was upset with myself for even getting on the plane. But now, I'm glad I'm here. I'm happy to be sitting across the table from this amazing woman and hopefully I'll be able to spend more time with her. I'd love to be able to spend Christmas with her, but I'm not sure if she already has plans. Either way, the possibility of seeing her and spending time with her while I'm here, I'm finally okay with being here for Christmas. In fact, I feel lucky. I'm hopeful for the future for the first time since my dad died and it's all because of Shea.

"You know," I begin, "this will be the first time that I'm spending Christmas away from my family," I admit.

She nods her head in understanding. "Me too. I think the strangest thing will be the weather," she claims.

My eyebrows draw down in confusion. "What do you mean?" I ask for clarification.

"It's going to be hot and sunny," she states the obvious.

"So?" I prod.

"So, no snow!" she emphasizes.

I nod my head, sympathetic. A lot of people love snow on Christmas, but we've had many cold Christmases without snow, making me appreciate the warm weather. What's a cold weather Christmas without the snow? I shrug like it's no big deal. "Hey, I'm okay with that. It's one less driveway I have to shovel," I grumble.

"I love the first snow," she proclaims. Her eyes light up with excitement. "My neighborhood looks like a postcard."

"Really?" I prod.

She nods her head in confirmation. "Yeah. You have to drive down this road before you turn onto my block and there are all of these trees with high branches that look like they are trying to hug each other over the pavement. When it snows, it creates this magical tunnel of white," she says animatedly, as she describes the scene in detail.

"Wow," I murmur in awe. "Are you sure you aren't a writer?" I prompt.

She laughs in response. The light sound sends chills down my spine. "It's how I see everything, like a photograph," she explains. She shrugs her shoulders like it's no big deal, but I don't see it as anything less than an incredible talent.

"The people here have been celebrating Christmas without snow forever," I remind her. "Just look at the decorations," I emphasize, gesturing around the room. Everywhere we look there's beautiful Christmas decorations, enhancing the holiday atmosphere from garland and wreaths, to stockings and lights, to trees and candy canes. They have it classically decorated with a little bit of a different look when you make your way around the resort from area to area.

She pastes a smile on her face and nods her head in acknowledgement. "I know. It's beautiful," she concedes. "It's just not," she grimaces and trails off, shrugging again.

"Home," I finish for her. I offer her an empathetic smile. She nods in agreement and smiles back at me. "Yeah, I get it," I concede.

"I know. I can tell," she murmurs, appreciatively.

"Do you have any plans for Christmas?" I prompt, hopeful.

She shakes her head in response. "Not anymore," she reveals, scrunching up her nose adorably in annoyance. "Kristen and I were supposed to go to some festival," she mumbles.

"Well, why don't we do something together?" I propose. I hold my breath, waiting for her answer.

"We?" she probes, arching her eyebrows in surprise. "As in me and you?" she reiterates, gesturing back and forth between us.

I feel my face heat and I exhale slowly, attempting to maintain my calm demeanor. "Yeah," I confirm, nodding my head as the corners of my lips twitch up.

She smiles brightly and the gesture alone causes me to sigh in relief. "Yes, I'd like that," she agrees.

"Great," I murmur.

"Do I have to wait until Christmas to see you?" she teases.

My heart skips a beat and I question, "Huh?"

"Well," she begins, "Christmas is four days away. Why don't we do all of the touristy things that we were going to do with Kristen and Daryl with each other instead," she proposes.

A smile tugs at the corners of my mouth. That's exactly what Daryl had suggested we do. I have his whole honeymoon package, including an array of things to do he already paid for. Now she's the one suggesting we go sightseeing together. "You sure you want to spend your vacation with me?" I prompt, playfully. "I mean, you just met me," I tease.

"That depends," she replies, playing along.

"On?" I probe.

"Well, do you want to spend your vacation with me?" she inquires.

I feel my face heat and I give her a crooked smile. "Well," I utter, dragging out the word.

She arches her eyebrows in challenge at my hesitation. "Don't forget I heard you on the phone with your brother," she reminds me.

I burst out laughing at her admission as the waitress steps up to our table. I guess she answered that question. "You got me there," I concede, not allowing my eyes to stray from Shea for even a moment.

"Would you like to charge this to your room?" the waitress inquires.

"Yes," we both declare, in unison.

"What is your room number?" she prompts.

I blurt out, "Four-oh-four."

At the same time, Shea states, "Four-oh-six."

The waitress looks back and forth between the two of us, slightly puzzled. Then, she shakes her head in amusement. She smirks and cautiously sets the bill down on the table between us. "I will just leave this here for you," she amends.

"Thank you," Shea replies.

The waitress walks away and Shea immediately puts her hand on the bill. I cover her hand with mine, causing electricity to shoot up my arm and send my heart into overdrive. I hold her hand and look into her eyes, wondering if she feels it too. "Let me," I request. I don't want her paying for our first date. I'm grateful she asked me out. I would've taken longer to do the same and I don't want to miss out on any time with her.

"No!" she exclaims, shaking her head. "I said I was buying you dinner," she insists.

"Shea, come on," I plead.

"Michael, that fall could have ended my life," she reminds me, making me flinch. Just the thought of something happening to her twists my stomach into knots. Saving her life should not be a reason for her to pay for our dinner.

I nod my head in acknowledgment and gulp down the lump in my throat. Then I look into her eyes, hoping she sees the sincerity in them as I speak. "Yeah," I concur, "but jumping after you started mine," I proclaim, vehemently.

She gasps and her eyes widen at my comment. I can see the questions running through her eyes and I want her to see the truth in mine. She tries to pull her hand away, but I give hers a squeeze and hold on tight. Does she feel this strong connection between us; the one I'm feeling for her? The feeling almost overwhelms me. She shakes her head as if brushing off my comment. She laughs awkwardly and fidgets in her seat. "You must say that to all the girls you rescue," she mumbles.

"I'm serious, Shea," I declare, pleading. I need her to understand how much she already means to me. I don't think I understand how, I just know that she does. "I'm terrified of heights," I emphasize. "When I saw you in the water," I pause, taking a deep breath to calm the anxiety eating at my insides as the memory runs through my mind. "I didn't even hesitate. I just jumped," I enlighten her. "I was supposed to come on this trip because I was supposed to meet you," I confidently claim, holding her gaze. As the words leave my lips, I can feel the truth in them in every part of me. My heart pounds erratically as I wait for her response.

"Okay, okay," she concedes. "You can pay the bill. But you have to go sightseeing with me tomorrow," she announces.

I grin, thrilled with her proposal. That's not a compromise. "Why don't you twist my arm a little?" I tease. She pretends to twist my arm with her free hand and I play along, faking the pain. "Ah! Easy," I mumble. I reluctantly release her hand and she quickly drops her hands back into her lap. I instantly feel the loss of her delicate touch. "Okay, have it your way," I easily relent.

"Good," she agrees.

I pick up the bill from the table and open it. Grabbing the pen, I quickly fill out the receipt. I snap the leather case closed and wave to the waitress to let her know it's ready for her. She smiles and nods her head in acknowledgement. I turn back to Shea and grin. "Thanks," I mumble, grateful she conceded.

She giggles softly in response. "Thank you," she emphasizes. "Ready to go?" she prods.

I reluctantly nod my head in agreement. I stand and walk around to her side. She rises and I hold my hand out, gesturing for her to lead the way out of the restaurant. I reluctantly follow, wishing this night didn't have to end.

We make it to our rooms, much too quickly. Shea turns and leans with her back against the door of her room. She looks up at me from underneath her long eyelashes, causing my heart to race. I lean down, drawn to her and she tips her head up towards me. I begin closing the distance, barely breathing, but I stop myself. I don't know if kissing her yet is the right thing. Something about this thing between us feels like so much more and I don't want to ruin it by jumping in too fast.

"What's wrong?" Shea prompts.

"Well, I have to confess," I begin, "I kind of want to kiss you," I admit, giving her a crooked smile.

She arches her eyebrows in question. "Kind of?" she prods.

I nod my head in confirmation, "Yeah, because I kind of don't."

Her eyebrows draw down in confusion adorably and her cheeks turn pink, while I fight a laugh. "I don't know if I should be insulted or not," she mumbles.

I quickly explain, not wanting her to get the wrong idea. "I don't want this night to end, but if we start kissing, it might end in a way neither one of us is ready for," I murmur.

She takes a deep breath and exhales slowly. "I see," she mumbles.

"Am I being too corny?" I prompt. I've never been like this with a girl, but there's something that keeps telling me I need to treat everything about Shea differently. I don't want to push her away.

She shakes her head and her cheeks turn a beautiful shade of pink. "No. You're being honest," she states. "I should be honest too," she acknowledges.

My whole body tenses at her comment. I should've known better. Someone like her cannot be single. "You have a boyfriend," I guess.

Her eyebrows draw down in confusion. "What? No!" she exclaims.

I breathe a sigh of relief. "Oh, good." I hesitate before I push, "Fiancé?"

"No!" she proclaims, shaking her head.

"Husband?" I ask as an afterthought. I might as well be clear.

"Heck no!" she states, giggling.

"Okay, phew, proceed," I grin.

Shea laughs in response, the light, carefree sound sending shivers down my spine. As she catches her breath she admits, "I don't want this night to end either. This has been the most amazing day of my life," she announces.

My breath catches in my throat and I gulp hard, quickly shaking it off. "Even falling?" I challenge.

"Especially falling," she emphasizes, taking me by surprise. "I never would have done something like that on purpose."

I huff a laugh and concede, "I never thought I would either."

"Seriously, though. We don't know where life is going to take us once we get home," she states. The thought of not seeing her after we leave here makes my stomach twist and my heart sink. I keep my lips pressed tightly together, waiting for her to elaborate. "I just want to remember this night as being perfect," she proclaims.

"So do I," I agree.

"Goodnight, Michael," she whispers.

"Goodnight, Shea," I rasp.

Neither one of us moves an inch, still lost in each other's gaze, causing both of us to begin fighting a smile. "Goodnight," she repeats.

"Night," I reply.

"Okay, how about a hug?" she suggests.

I nod my head in agreement, "Yeah, a hug is good."

She steps towards me and circles her arms around my neck, while my arms immediately wrap around her back. She settles onto my shoulder as I pull her close, my body heating and my heart racing. My head falls into the crook of her neck and I take a deep breath, inhaling her sweet scent. She fits perfectly in my arms. It feels like this is exactly where she's supposed to be. "Uh-oh," I mumble into the side of her head.

"What?" she prompts.

"We have an even bigger problem," I declare.

"What's that?" she asks.

"I don't want to let go," I reply honestly.

She giggles and pulls away. I reluctantly let my hands fall to my sides, releasing her. "Goodnight, Nine-C. For real this time," she grins.

"For real," I concur." She slips her key into her lock and opens the door. "Goodnight," I repeat.

"Goodnight," she reiterates and closes the door behind her.

I smile to myself as I unlock my own door and slip inside. "What have I gotten myself into?" I grin. Shea has definitely taken me by surprise.

Chapter 15

Shea

I glance down at my outfit as I make my way down to the restaurant for breakfast. I want to look good, but I also want to be comfortable for sightseeing. It's warm today, but not too hot. I'm wearing worn gray jeans a white tank top and a thin crop sweater with a flower design in the weave over the top. I slip on my simple white slides, knowing they're comfortable for walking and we might be doing a lot of that today. I have just the very top of my hair pulled back and away from my face, with the rest of it hanging straight over my shoulders.

I walk into the restaurant and the hostess nods at me in greeting, recognizing me from yesterday. I give her a small wave and smile. Then, I walk through the restaurant looking for Michael, but it doesn't look like he's here yet. I find an empty table for two in the back near and set my bag down. Then, I make my way over to the buffet and make up a plate for myself with a veggie omelet and a cup of strawberry yogurt with some granola to stir in. I grab an orange juice and coffee, adding a little cream and sugar. Balancing everything in my hands and arms, I'm careful as I cautiously return to the table. I set everything down and then decide to walk back to the bar to get coffee and juice for Michael too before I sit down to wait for him. Taking a bite of my breakfast, I glance down at my phone to check my messages while I wait.

Tapping on a message from Kristen, I read, "I'm still waiting to hear from you! I want to know how your date went!"

I grin and reply, "My date went well. Having breakfast now and then we're going to head out to do some sight-seeing today."

"We?!?" she exclaims.

Giggling softly to myself, I respond, "Yes, we. I'll tell you all about it later."

"Always, later," she grumbles. "Okay, I guess I can wait. Have fun!"

"Thank you!" I answer.

Sam steps up to the table just as I set my phone down and take a bite of my breakfast. "Good morning, Miss Shea," he greets me.

I look up, covering my mouth as I swallow the food in my mouth, before I drop my hand to my lap and return his friendly smile. "Good morning, Sam," I reply, cheerfully.

He tilts his head to the side and narrows his eyes, assessing me. "You look different this morning," he comments.

I huff a laugh and nod my head in agreement. "I'm not so jet-lagged anymore," I claim, remembering how tired I felt most of my first day.

He shakes his head, still looking thoughtful. "No, no, it's something else," he mumbles. "You're glowing," he declares, smiling wide.

I laugh in response. "Glowing?" I question. "Me?" I reiterate, gesturing to myself and arching my eyebrows in challenge.

He nods his head in affirmation. "Yes. If you didn't tell me you were single, I would think you were in love," I he proclaims.

I gasp as my eyes widen, a little stunned by his statement and not quite sure how to even respond. I'm definitely not in love. I can't be. I feel my face heat at the thought. I just met Michael, but I can admit I like him and

I'm interested. I open my mouth to reply to Sam, when Michael steps up to the table and greets me, interrupting my train of thought. "Good morning!" he announces. He sets a plate of food down on the table and then slips his black backpack off and sets it down on the floor next to him, before sitting down in the chair across from me. He's dressed in dark jeans, a short-sleeved pale gray shirt with two buttons at his collar and navy blue on the sleeves as well as along the collar. "Sorry I'm late," he immediately apologizes to me. Then, he turns his attention to Sam and declares, "Good morning, Sam."

Sam's smile grows as he nods to Michael in acknowledgement. "And a very good morning to you too, Sir." Sam gives me a knowing look, appearing almost giddy. I shrug my shoulders in response, while my face heats almost instantly.

Michael looks back and forth between Sam and me, a puzzled look on his face. "What?" he finally probes.

Sam shakes his head in answer and claims, "Nothing at all." He attempts to shake off his excitement and clears his throat before he continues. "Enjoy your day," he encourages, giving us both a nod.

"Thank you, Sam," I reply. I feel a little flushed, grateful Sam doesn't say anything to Michael. I'm not sure what he would think.

He walks away whistling what sounds like the same song the guitarist was playing the other night, bringing a smile to my face at the memory.

Michael glances at the table, noticing the additional juice and coffee for the first time. "Is this for me?" he asks with a crooked grin.

"Yes," I confirm, shrugging like it's no big deal. "I thought I'd help out since I got here before you," I claim.

"Thank you," he acknowledges. "That was very thoughtful."

"You're welcome," I murmur. I smile across the table at him, as I pick up my cup and take a sip of my orange juice.

"So, what would you like to do today?" Michael inquires.

I feel the excitement building inside of me at the thought of everything I want to see today. We don't have a lot of time and I want to fit as much in as possible. "There's so much to do and see here. Look!" I exclaim. I pull the guidebook out of the top of my bag and flip it around towards Michael so he can see what I'm talking about. I point to the different things as I talk animatedly. "There are castles and ruins and temples and all sorts of natural landmarks. You can even drive from one side of the island to the other," I ramble.

He smirks and chuckles softly. "Slow down, Shea," he requests, interrupting me. "We've got plenty of time," he emphasizes.

I glance at my wrist, looking at the time. "It's already eight-thirty and the sun goes down at about seven. That's already less than twelve hours," I emphasize.

He chuckles softly and shakes his head. Shrugging his shoulders, he enlightens me, "I'm here until the thirtieth."

I look up at him with wide eyes, my heart suddenly racing. I thought he only agreed to go sightseeing with me for today. I wanted to try to squeeze as much in as possible while we were going exploring together, but this might change things. "So am I," I reply, hopeful.

"Do we really need to see everything in one day," he prompts. "Or can we take our time?" he requests.

Does he really want to start by committing so much time to me? "You want to spend your whole vacation with me?" I clarify.

He shrugs in answer, the corners of his lips tugging upwards. "Why not?" he prods.

"We just met," I reiterate, as if he doesn't know. He may change his mind after spending the day with me today, or even after just a couple hours.

"Oh, I'm sorry. Do you have someone else you'd prefer to spend your vacation with?" he taunts, arching his eyebrows in challenge.

"Well," I begin, dragging out the word. I don't know how to tell him what I'm thinking without just coming out and saying it.

He chuckles and shakes his head in amusement. "Let me rephrase that," he asserts, his green eyes sparkling like emeralds. "Is there anyone else on this island that you'd prefer to spend your vacation with?" he prompts.

I smirk and answer him playfully. "Well, Sam does seem a bit committed to his job," I joke, trailing off.

"Hey, now," he grumbles, feigning offense.

I pause and take a deep breath, exhaling slowly as I gather my courage. "Honestly, Michael, I don't want you to feel obligated to hang out with me," I explain. "If you don't want to go today," I begin, trying to give him a way out. I've really been looking forward to going with him today, but I don't want to force him into spending time with me either, especially if he'd rather be doing something else.

He interrupts me before I can finish my suggestion. "Who said I don't want to go?" he challenges. "Shea, I like you. You're fun to be with. I really want to get to know you," he claims. I look into his eyes, seeing nothing, but sincerity.

I feel my face heat and my heart skips a beat, as I smile across the table at him. "I'd like to get to know you too," I admit.

"So, what's the problem?" he questions. I open my mouth to respond, but he continues before I'm able to speak. "Look, maybe this will turn into something and maybe it won't. Let's just take it day by day and have fun finding out," he suggests.

My heart gets stuck in my throat, so I nod my head in response, not yet able to speak. I gulp hard, forcing my heart back into my chest. Then, I lick my suddenly dry lips so I'm able to talk. Trying again, I concur, "That sounds like a good plan."

He grins at my response. "Plus, my brother has all of these excursions and tours booked," he informs me. Reaching down into his backpack, he pulls a large blue envelope out, holding it in front of him. "He can't get his money back and told me to use them all. They're all for two people, so..." he pauses, looking around the restaurant, "I could probably find someone who might want to use them," he taunts.

I gasp and my eyes widen in excitement. "Shut up!" I laugh and reach across the table, attempting to snatch the envelope out of his hand.

He pulls it back, holding it just out of my reach and questions playfully, "What? Would you like to use them? With me?"

"Yes!" I proclaim, instantly agreeing and practically bouncing in my seat in anticipation.

He laughs at my reaction. "Yeah?" he prods.

"Absolutely!" I confirm.

He holds the envelope out towards me, grinning in satisfaction. I quickly snatch it out of his hands with a small squeal of excitement. I begin flipping through all the reservations, my eagerness growing by the second. "I'll take that as a maybe," he jokes, chuckling softly.

I laugh along with him as I continue skimming through all the papers in the envelope. My eyes stop on a couple's spa appointment, including a couple's massage and I gasp. "We get to go to the spa!" I announce, giddily.

"We do?" he questions in surprise.

I laugh at his reaction and shake my head in disbelief. "Did you even look at this?" I prompt.

He shrugs his shoulders like it's no big deal. "No. When I was going with Daryl, I figured he would just tell me what we were doing and when and then when I got on the plane alone, I didn't know if I would be doing any of it," I concede.

"We have to do all of this! This is fantastic!" I proclaim. I feel myself blush a deep shade of red. I shrug my shoulders, attempting to contain my exuberance. "Well, that is if you want to keep hanging out with me," I amend.

He chuckles and feigning exasperation, he reminds me, "Didn't we just talk about this?" I blush again as I nod my head and shrug my shoulders in response. He looks into my eyes, his own turning serious as he leans across the table towards me and emphasizes, "Shea, I'm not changing my mind anytime soon. You're stuck with me, now."

His words send shockwaves to my heart, making it stutter in my chest. My stomach twists into knots as butterflies take over, spreading tingles throughout my body, and causing goosebumps to erupt over my skin. Taking a deep breath, I exhale slowly, attempting to calm my sudden nerves. What is this guy doing to me?

Chapter 16

Shea

I sit in the back seat of a car with Michael by my side, taking in the beautiful scenery as it passes us by. I lean towards Michael, looking over him to see out the window at the water down below, just over the rocky cliff. The water is so blue, but it ranges from dark blues, to light blues, to aqua, teal and shades of green. I glance up at him and see he's staring at me, instead of out the window, making me blush. I sit back in my seat and prod, "What?" feeling a little self-conscious. "The view is incredible," I add, gesturing out his window.

"I'd rather watch you enjoying the view than out the window at the height we're at right now," he admits.

I feel my face turn a deeper shade of red, even though part of his comment stems from his fear of heights. Then again, seeing him so anxious just reminds me again of the other day when he saved my life without hesitating. "Well, if that's the case, keep looking at me until we get to the castle," I propose, attempting to comfort him. "Seeing you like this, I really can't believe you jumped off a cliff for me," I admit, acknowledging his sacrifice.

"I'd do it for you again in a heartbeat," he declares, vehemently.

My breath hitches and my heart skips a beat. Clearing my throat, I ask, "Have you ever visited any other countries?" I hope the change in subject will help to distract him.

He smiles at me in appreciation, knowing what I'm trying to do. The rest of the ride to our first destination, I relax back into my seat and watch him. I find myself learning more about him than I do about where we're going.

I struggle to catch my breath from laughter, as we pull into a gravel parking lot. "We're here," the driver announces. We both glance out the window and look up. We're parked in front of a large structure that looks like a square castle. It has red stone in front with towers on each corner of the structure. The base of the building has a wall of rocks built up around it like an additional wall of both support and protection. I'm so excited to see what it looks like up close. We step out of the car and I immediately pull out my camera. Holding it up, I swiftly make a few adjustments on my settings, before I start taking pictures.

"Already at it, huh?" Michael prods as he walks around the car, standing by my side. He glances down at the viewfinder and arches his eyebrows in surprise. "Wow, that's really good. It's so vivid," he mumbles. He glances up at the building in front of us and then he looks back at my camera. "Wow," he mumbles in awe.

I grin, my heart skipping a beat as I quietly appreciate his compliment. "Come on, let's go," I encourage.

We walk side by side up to a set of steep stone steps. He stops to read the sign, providing information about the structure. "Saint Agatha's Tower or The Red Tower," he reads.

"That's appropriate," I mumble.

He grins and continues reading as I snap a few pictures. "It was built around 1649 and it was basically a military defense tower, storing supplies and shooting cannons and guns to protect them from enemies during wars," he informs me. Glancing out at the sea, I have to admit, it's an excellent viewpoint for enemies coming in

141

from almost anywhere. "There's even a chapel inside," he adds as an afterthought.

I begin walking up the stairs and he follows, quickly catching up to me and even passing me as I snap picture after picture. "You okay?" he prods, as I begin to fall behind.

I nod my head in acknowledgement, "Yeah, I'm just taking a few pictures along the way. I'll catch up if I fall behind," I insist.

He nods in acknowledgement before he turns, taking his time walking up the stairs and glancing back to check on me every few steps. I continue to stop, taking more pictures. I can't help it. As Michael looks around, I turn my lens towards him. I snap a few pictures of him, unnoticed and smile to myself. A few minutes later I look up just as Michael jogs the last few steps down towards me, coming back for me and making me laugh. He leans in towards me, putting his head next to mine and holds his phone out in front of the two of us. I smile as he quickly snaps a selfie of the two of us and then offers me a mischievous grin. "I didn't want to miss that one," he proclaims. I laugh in response. "Come on," he prods.

I follow him up to the castle and look up in awe. "Wow," I mumble and take a few more pictures. "It's crazy to think of all the bad things that probably happened right here, especially during the wars," I mumble.

"Yeah, it is," he concurs.

When we reach the top, I watch as he takes a deep breath, exhaling slowly. I reach out and grasp his hand, giving it a light squeeze in encouragement. Glancing down at me, he smiles in appreciation, making sure not to get too close to the edge.

After just a little while longer, we make our way back to the car and the driver drops us off at a more elaborate castle known as the Citadel or the Gran Castello.

Stepping out onto a cobblestone street, we look up at the interconnected buildings. The stone structure appears to be in various shades of tan and looks to continue on and on like a maze. I notice several towers, turrets and steeples, making me excited to see more.

We make our way inside and I'm instantly overwhelmed with its beauty. The high ceilings, ornate lighting, the paintings and an enormous mural, all with intricate details in everything I see. Michael pulls out our tickets from Daryl's folder and hands them to the attendant standing guard. We show our passports and then we're finally allowed entry.

We stroll down the hallway, reading about traditional lifestyle in the agrarian economy of the Maltese islands, as well as several crafts, skills and traditions that helped shaped daily life here over the years. We find information telling us the architecture of the buildings was based in Sicilian style, and influenced by fourteenth century Counts of Malta, although the museum section of the castle where we are now was built in the sixteenth century, utilizing a cluster of houses that were later rehabilitated as the museum.

I snap a few more pictures before I return the lens cover back to my camera and let it hang over my shoulder, trying to just enjoy the moment. Walking with Michael side by side, I find my heart in my throat and my fingers tingling in anticipation with him so close. The back of his fingertips brush mine and I have a quick intake of breath at the contact. A moment later, I gather my courage and slip my hand into his. I smile to myself as he allows his fingers to entwine with mine. He gives my hand a gentle squeeze, sending goosebumps up my arms and tingles to consume my insides. We slowly continue down the hallway, admiring the interior of the castle as our hands swing casually back and forth between us.

We finally make our way out of the castle, but instead of getting back in a car, we decide to walk for a little while, enjoying the scenery and the gorgeous weather. We amble down the hill and begin following the road along the shore, taking pictures as we go. We come across an adorable outdoor café with a beautiful view of the Mediterranean Sea, as well as a couple swimming pools down below. Turning towards me, he questions, "Are you hungry?" I nod my head and he adds, "Would you like to try here for lunch?"

"I'd love to," I concur, nodding in agreement. We sit down at a table overlooking the sea and the pools. Just like on our balcony at the resort, there's a clear glass barrier, giving us a clear view of the scenery. "This is so beautiful," I murmur. "Everything is," I amend, glancing back across the table at Michael.

"It really is," he agrees, continuing to stare at me and bringing the color back to my cheeks once again.

A young waitress steps up to the table with her long brown hair braided down her back. She smiles politely and says, "Hello! May I get you both something to drink?"

My stomach growls in response and I request, "Is it okay if we order?"

"Of course," she agrees. "What can I get you?"

What feels like only a few minutes later, I'm nearly done with my rice bowl with a white fish similar to Mahi-Mahi and topped with fresh mango salsa. "Mm," I mumble, the sweet and savory flavors bursting in my mouth.

"That looks really good," he acknowledges.

"Would you like to try a bite?" I offer.

"Sure," he agrees. I pick up a forkful and hold it up towards him. Instead of taking the fork from me, he leans forward and bites it right off my fork, making me smile. I watch him as he closes his eyes and mumbles his own appreciation, "Mm." He opens his eyes and holds my gaze. "That's really good," he claims.

I nod my head in agreement, smiling at him. Setting my fork down, I inquire, "So what are we doing next?"

"Well, it looks like St. John's Co-Cathedral is close by?" he suggests.

"That sounds perfect," I concur.

The waitress steps up to our table and states, "I'll take this when you are ready." She sets down a small, rectangular, black leather case, leaving us with our bill.

"Thank you," I tell her.

Michael swipes it up and slips his money inside. I give him a look and he grins like it's no big deal. "Ready?" he prompts.

I relent, shaking my head as I stand. He places his hand on the small of my back as we exit, my skin on fire at his touch. Then, he immediately grasps my hand and clasps it in his, as we turn down the street, side by side.

As we enter the courtyard at the cathedral, I realize I haven't done a vlog yet today. I inform him, "I should do a quick vlog for my site. Do you mind?"

"Of course not," he states, making me laugh.

"Quite the change of heart," I tease him.

Stepping closer he stops me and looks down at me, his gaze intense. "I'd have to agree with that," he concedes.

My heart skips a beat and I struggle to breathe as I stare into his eyes. I force myself to take a deep breath and tear my gaze away from his. Pulling my phone out, I hold it up and tap to record. "Hi, everyone! I've been doing some sight seeing today around Malta with Michael otherwise known as Nine-C, here," I announce.

Turning the phone just enough to see Michael standing over my shoulder, he grins and waves, seeming bashful. "Hi!"

"Michael and I have been touring castles and museums today and let me tell you everything has been absolutely incredible. I'll be sure to post some of my pictures on my website when I get home, so you'll have to wait until then. But to give you a little taste of the architecture, right now we're standing in front of St. John's Co-Cathedral." I spin around slowly, making sure to take in some of my surroundings. "Hope you like that little taste and I promise to share more soon. In the meantime, remember to check in to follow my story every day to continue getting updates of what I'm doing. It's definitely been an amazing day!" I exclaim. "Well, Ciao for now!" I blow a kiss to the camera and tap to end the video. I quickly upload it as we continue down the road, not wanting to waste a minute of my time with Michael.

I glance up at him, tapping away on his phone. "Are you ready to go inside?" I inquire.

"Almost," he mumbles and continues tapping. Then, he looks up at me and grins as he slips his phone back in his pocket. "Okay, let's go see some skeletons."

Giggling, I correct, "It's just depictions of skeletons as a reminder of the deaths of several Knights and other important people." I look at him with curiosity, wondering what he was doing, but I don't ask.

He puts me out of my misery, explaining, "I just had to follow this girl's vlog on her website before I forget. I've heard she's beautiful, amazing to watch and she's an incredible photographer too," he proclaims.

I grin, feeling my face heat with the compliment. "Well, I'm sure she appreciates that," I murmur, playing along. He tugs my hand, urging me along.

After a lot of walking, numerous pictures and even a little bit of shopping in some of the local shops, we decide to make our way back to the resort. We get back in plenty of time to make our dinner reservation. We sit outside, enjoying our dinner on the restaurant terrace. I spot the guitarist playing again, both inside and out, but this time, Michael needs no encouragement to ask me to dance. He holds out his hand for me and I take it, holding his gaze. He pulls me into his arms and we spend the rest of the night dancing, laughing and talking. Everything just feels so natural and electric with him causing the night to feel like it's flying by.

I'm reluctant for the night to end, but if we're going to go sightseeing again tomorrow, it has to. Michael and I stroll back to our rooms, taking our time. He stops in front of my door and turns to me. "Thank you for today. I had so much fun," I reveal.

"You don't need to thank me," he insists. "I had the best time with you today. Thank you," he emphasizes.

He steps towards me and wraps me up in his warm embrace, making my heartbeat quicken. I wrap my arms around his back and hug him tightly feeling happy, giddy and content. As I feel his hold loosen, I reluctantly let him go and take a step back. "Goodnight," I state.

"Goodnight, Shea," he replies with a heart-melting smile.

I unlock my door and slip inside, with a huge grin on my face. I put my hand on the door handle, wanting to pull it open again. I push up on my tiptoes and peak out the peephole instead. My eyes widen in surprise as I notice Michael, still standing outside my door. I hold my breath, waiting to see what he'll do. He finally takes a step back and moves just out of range. Only a moment later, I hear the muffled sound of his door clicking shut on the other side of my wall. "Goodnight, Michael," I repeat as I finally release my breath.

Chapter 17

Michael

I drink the last of my orange juice as I sit at the same table as yesterday at the resort restaurant with Shea, making our plans for the day. "We have reservations tonight at the restaurant downtown," I remind her.

"I can't wait," she mumbles her acknowledgement. "That's the restaurant that's supposed to have exceptional food, a great view with outdoor seating and then they have dancing on the lower level that extends out onto a beach," she elaborates.

"It does sound incredible," I concur. "I can't wait to dress up and take you out on the town," I grin.

She laughs and shakes her head in amusement. "Okay," she murmurs, her cheeks turning a beautiful shade of pink. I'm beginning to love that color on her.

Sam walks by and smiles at both of us, interrupting her thought. "Good morning, Miss Shea. Good morning, Mr. Michael," he states happily and continues on, greeting the other guests.

"Good morning, Sam," we both call to his retreating back.

"Do you want to start at the Valetta Tunnels and then make our way to the upside-down?" I propose.

"The upside down?" she questions.

"It was formed from a sinkhole caused by an earthquake or storm or something and the trees actually grow upside down off the cliff," I explain.

"You want to go near another cliff?" she challenges.

"No," I reply honestly, the corners of my lips twitching up in amusement, "but I thought you might."

She puts her hand to her chest, as if attempting to calm her racing heart bringing a smile to my face. "How about we check out some of the tunnels and then we just make our way into downtown to do some shopping," she suggests instead.

I smile in appreciation and nod my head in agreement. "Sounds good," I concur. "Ready?" I prompt.

"Yes," she agrees and pushes back from the table, standing up.

I follow her through the restaurant and outside. We don't have to wait to get into another van. The driver pulls out of the resort and turns in the opposite direction than he did yesterday. As we cruise down the street, we begin pointing out different things that draw our attention. I find myself spotting things I think she might like pictures of and point them out, even if it's just for her. I want to do things for her to bring a smile to her face.

It doesn't take long before we make it to one of the entrances of the tunnels. Watching as Shea snaps pictures, I pull out my phone. Tapping on my camera, I flip it around and lean close to Shea, "Smile," I announce and take a selfie of the two of us. "Thanks," I mumble as I assess the picture, my smile growing. She's so beautiful and I look happy again.

"Will you send it to me?" she requests.

"Of course," I agree. I send the picture to her and then to Darryl right after, tapping out a message to him. "Sightseeing with Shea." I press send and my phone beeps almost instantly, but I ignore it, focusing on the woman beside me as I reach for her hand.

We take our time strolling through the tunnels and some ruins, Shea constantly stopping to take pictures, several with me in them. She holds the camera up, ready to take another picture and I stand in front of her, blocking her view. Laughing, she states the obvious, "I can't see what I'm trying to take a picture of, Michael."

Smirking, I nod my head and carefully grab the camera. "It's my turn to get a picture of you," I advise.

She grins, agreeing instantly, "Okay. I'm rarely ever in pictures." She steps next to me, the sweet scent of her instantly filling my senses. Reaching up, she adjusts the settings to make it easier on me to take her picture before she releases the camera back over to me. She steps away from me and I grimace feeling the loss, even though she's right in front of me.

"It definitely shouldn't be that way," I claim. I snap a picture of her and then, she poses, holding her hands out as if displaying everything around her. Chuckling I snap a few more pictures, grateful they all seem to be in focus this time. "Looks good, I think."

"You got it this time?" she teases, making me laugh. Giggling sweetly, she steps towards me and quickly sifts through the pictures I just took. "Not bad," she praises.

"Thanks," I mumble, hearing the pride in my own voice.

An older couple, both with gray hair, saunters by hand in hand as they look around. Shea calls out to them, getting their attention. "Excuse me."

They both stop and look at her curiously. "Would you mind taking a picture of the two of us?" she requests. "We don't really have any good ones of the two of us together," she explains.

"Of course," the woman smiles and the couple steps closer to us. Shea changes some settings and gives them both basic instructions on what to do.

"Do you mind?" she prompts with a questioning arch of her brow, making me laugh.

"I'd be honored," I claim. She steps over to me and slings her arm around my waist, bringing an even bigger smile to my face. I lift my arm over her shoulder and gently pull her close to me, feeling like that's where she's meant to be. We both glance at one another and smile before forcing our focus towards the camera grinning.

After a few moments, the woman holds the camera out to Shea and proposes, "Do you want to look at them to make sure they're okay?"

She steps away from me and I immediately feel the loss of her warmth. "I'm sure they'll be fine," Shea proclaims. "Thank you."

"You're welcome," she acknowledges. "You two remind me of my husband and I when we were your age," she claims grinning. "You can't seem to take your eyes off each other."

My chest tightens as I watch Shea's cheeks turn a beautiful shade of pink at the woman's comment. "Have a good day," she rasps.

"Thank you," I add. I am grateful we'll have more than just a selfie together from this trip. She's the one that's making every minute memorable.

As we leave the ruins, we find a small coffee shop with some outdoor seating. "Would you like to stop for a few minutes?" I suggest.

"Sure," she agrees.

We make our way inside and order two specialty coffees. "If you would like to go sit down, the waitress can bring your order out to you, the barista offers.

"Thank you," I acknowledge.

We step through the side door and find dark wicker couches and chairs with thick ivory cushions and matching end tables with a glass top. Palms, a few tropical flowers and other lush tropical greenery surround the whole area, helping maintain its privacy. "This is really pretty," she comments as we sit down together on the couch.

Only a few minutes later the waitress steps outside, setting down two white coffee cups. Glancing inside at the mug, the milk whipped at the top is accented with a mocha powdered heart making me chuckle. "Wow, that takes talent," I comment.

"I love that," she murmurs, softly.

"Do you still wish Kristen were here with you?" I prod.

"Well," she begins, dragging out the word and making me laugh. She shrugs and concedes, "I miss her, sure," she pauses, hesitating momentarily, when I see a sudden look of determination flash in her eyes, "but I think I'm exploring Malta with the person I'm meant to be exploring Malta with." She blushes again and looks away.

"Shea," I prod and wait for her to meet my gaze. "I think I'm where I'm supposed to be and who I'm supposed to be with too." Her smile lights up her whole face at my admission. She breaks our gaze and I take a sip of the coffee, feeling the foam stick briefly to my upper lip, and grinning in amusement as it does the same to Shea.

We finish our coffees and spend the rest of the afternoon walking down the cobblestone streets into the small stores and shops. I love watching the excitement flooding Shea's face every time she finds something she thinks is unique. I spot an ice cream parlor and suggest, "Why don't we get some ice cream to tide us over until dinner?" I suggest. "Then, we can head back to the resort to get ready before we go out to dinner."

"I'm up for ice cream," she agrees. We walk inside and get in line. "What's your favorite?" she inquires.

"That's a tough question," I claim. "I guess I'm more of a vanilla person, but I like cookies and cream, sweet cream and a few others."

"So as long as it's at least somewhat white?" she teases.

Chuckling, I nod my head and mutter, "Something like that. I guess if I'm going to have toppings on my ice cream, I want to add them myself."

"Really?" she probes, surprised.

I smirk and admit, "Well, yeah. Isn't adding the toppings half the fun of ice cream?" I question, arching my eyebrow in challenge.

"I don't know about that. I think eating it is the best part," she claims.

Chuckling, I concur, "Well, I can't argue with you there. What about you? What's your favorite flavor of ice cream?"

"Probably strawberry, but I like most of the fruity flavors and every once in a while I like something with chocolate," she answers. "I think I'll go with the fresh strawberry today," she decides. She orders a strawberry cone and I order vanilla. She holds out her hand and pays before I realize what she's doing.

As we walk outside with our ice cream and begin making our way down the street, just enjoying being together, I turn to her and mumble, "Thank you for the ice cream."

"I had to do something to pay you back for jumping off a cliff for me," she teases.

Laughing, I ask, "Am I ever going to live that down?"

"What? Saving my life or your fear of heights?" she asks.

"Well, I guess it doesn't matter, both brought me to you," I mumble.

She gives me a look, making me laugh again. "That was a little bit corny," she claims, holding her fingers closely together in demonstration.

"Even if it's true?" I push. My face begins to hurt from smiling and laughing so much today. I don't want our time together to end.

She blushes, her cheeks turning so pink, they nearly match her ice cream. She yawns, attempting to hide it behind her hand.

"Are you going to make it to dinner tonight?" I inquire.

"Absolutely," she confirms.

Shaking my head in amusement, I toss the remainder of our cones and get us a van back to the resort. She climbs into the back next to me and the driver barely pulls away from the side of the road before Shea falls asleep on my shoulder. Glancing down at her, I grin and wrap my arm around her, pulling her close. She settles into my embrace, fitting perfectly in my arms. I look down at her, admiring her beauty and appreciating every moment I get to spend with her. I've never felt so lucky. She nuzzles even closer to me in her sleep, causing my heart to skip a beat. I tilt my head down towards hers and close my eyes, more than happy and content. I feel alive.

We pull up to the hotel and I glance down at her, reluctant to wake her up, but I know I have to. "Shea," I urge her gently. Her eyes flutter open and she lifts her tired gaze to mine. The look on her face only makes me want to carry her to her room to help her. "We're back at the resort," I whisper.

She nods her head and carefully untangles herself from my arms, while I grudgingly let her go. We walk slowly to our rooms, hand in hand. I stop in front of her door and pull her into my arms, giving her a hug and enjoying the feel of her there. She pulls back and gives me a tired smile. "Thank you for today," she mumbles. "I had a lot of fun."

"Me too, Shea," I agree.

"Are you sure you still want to go to dinner in town?" I question.

"We have to eat. Besides, a shower will help wake me up," she claims.

"We could always eat here tonight and make a plan to go there after Christmas," I suggest.

"No, let's go tonight," she reiterates.

"Okay," I concede, believing I may agree to almost anything when it comes to this woman. "I'll see you in a little while," I proclaim. She nods her head in acknowledgement. Then, I watch as she disappears inside her room. Smiling to myself, I return to my room. Every minute I spend with her, I'm increasingly more and more excited to find out what comes next. I've never felt like this before and I've only known her for a few days, but I'm already starting to believe she's my happily ever after. I just don't want to say anything too soon and scare her away.

Chapter 18

Shea

I glance in the mirror, dressed and ready for dinner. I'm attempting to go for a casual, but nice look wearing a simple white knit shirt with spaghetti straps that scoops in near my arms matched with simple black skinny jeans and my white slides. I left my hair down tonight, straightening it to get rid of any frizz and make it silky smooth. I'm feeling a little bit more awake than I did earlier, but I don't think I can do a late night tonight after so much walking around the last two days. It surprises me sometimes how much something so simple can make me so exhausted.

Reaching for my phone, I decide to do a quick vlog before I head out for the evening. Holding it up, I tap record and begin. "Good evening everyone! Well, it's evening here. I'm not sure what time it is there, back home I guess it's closer to lunchtime than anything. Anyway, Michael and I are about to head downtown to grab some dinner at a nice restaurant overlooking the Mediterranean Sea. We heard the menu is absolutely amazing and it's something not to be missed. Then, maybe after dinner, we were thinking we might do a little more dancing if I'm able to stay on my feet after that," I laugh. "After so much sightseeing the last couple days, my feet might not cooperate with me."

"Anyway, I'm grateful I've gotten this second chance to get to know Nine-C. He's not at all who I thought he was. In fact, he's almost the opposite of that person. He's pretty amazing," I murmur, trailing off. I straighten up and attempt to focus, "Anyway, hopefully I'll be able to update you tomorrow on what the nightlife in Malta is like, at least when it's so close to Christmas. Ciao, for now!" I state and tap to end the video before quickly uploading it to my site.

A knock on my door startles me, making me jump. Laughing at myself, I glance at my reflection one more time in the mirror before I grab my purse, slipping my phone and room key inside. He knocks again, just as I pull the door open, finding Michael on the other side taking my breath away. He looks incredibly handsome in tan pants and a soft blue button down dress shirt with the sleeves rolled up to his elbows. The blue shirt almost makes his green eyes look blue and brings a smile to my face. "Hi!" I murmur.

"Shea," he mumbles, shaking his head. "You look beautiful."

"Thank you," I reply, feeling my cheeks heat from his compliment. "You look pretty good yourself," I state.

"Thank you," he grins. "Are you ready to go?"

"Yes," I declare, holding up my bag as if it's the proof he needs. "Let's go."

Pulling my door shut behind me, we make our way downstairs and out to the front of the resort, finding a car already waiting to take us into town. "Did you plan this?" I ask.

"I just called down right before I left my room," he advises.

"Nice," I mumble, almost inaudibly.

It doesn't take long before we reach the restaurant and the view is even more than they could explain. Of course, part of the reason for that had to do with the indescribable sunset. Bright reds, oranges, yellows, blues and purples fill the sky, one color bleeding into the next. Michael leans on the rail next to our table, holding his arm out and gesturing for me to come closer.

"What?" I ask as I approach.

"You have to see the view from over here," he urges. "Everything from the sunset, to the sea, to the lights and buildings of the island," he pauses shaking his head in awe, "I don't think I've ever seen anything like it."

"Okay," I agree, closing the distance between us. He reaches his arm out for me and I stand in front of him, his hand resting gently on my shoulder. He leans down close to my face, until I feel his warm breath on my cheek giving me chills. He stretches his arm out over the railing, pointing out different places we've been to together in just the last couple days. I can't wipe the smile from my face and I don't want to. We stand there momentarily, enjoying our close proximity as the sun begins to set, watching until it almost disappears over the horizon.

He smiles down at me and I tilt my head up, looking at him over my shoulder. He gives me a look, making me wonder if this could be our moment. He tips his head a little closer to mine, his gaze moving from my eyes to my lips, as if asking permission. I push up a little taller on my toes and he begins closing the distance between us, my heart pounding erratically as I anticipate our first kiss.

"Excuse me," the waitress interjects as she arrives at our table. Her sudden arrival startles us both apart. I fall back on my heels, bumping into Michael. His hand falls to my elbow as he steadies us both. "Would you like anything to drink?" she inquires.

Exhaling slowly, I step away from Michael and walk around the table, sitting back down in my seat before I respond. "A glass of pinot noir, please," I request.

"I'll have the same," Michael states as he lowers himself into the seat across from me. "Thank you," he adds.

She nods firmly and emphasizes, "I'll be right back with your drinks." Then, she spins on her heel and stalks back inside the restaurant as if we were the ones interrupting her. I look at Michael with wide eyes, his expression mirroring my own, causing both of us to burst out laughing.

"So, tell me about your family," I begin, redirecting the conversation. "It seems like you and your brother are really close," I comment.

Nodding his head in agreement, he emphasizes, "We are. We've always been close. Of course we've had our moments," he grins, "but after everything we've been through this past year, I'd say he's my best friend."

"Here are your drinks," the waitress declares as she sets the two glasses down on the table in front of us.

"Thank you," we reply in unison.

"Are you ready to order?" she questions.

"Could we have a few more minutes to look at the menu?" I request. We keep getting so lost in each other that we haven't even thought about what to eat, but that's okay with me.

She gives us a tight smile and responds, "Of course."

We both reach for our menus and quickly scan through it, deciding what to order. "I think I'll go with the swordfish," he mumbles.

"Mm, that sounds good," I agree.

"If you'd like, we can always share our meals if you want to try something else?" he proposes. "That way we can try a couple things. Everything sounds so good!"

"I like that idea," I murmur, glancing back over the menu. "How does the Sea bass sound?" I prompt.

"I'd definitely have some. I don't think we can go wrong with fresh fish when we're on an island," he teases.

I laugh in response, just as the waitress returns to our table. "Are you ready to order now?" she probes.

Grinning, with his smile making me feel weak, he answers, "Yes, we're going to have the swordfish and sea bass."

"Excellent choices. Thank you," she replies and turns back towards the kitchen to place our orders.

"So," he begins, "tell me more about your family," he requests. We spend the rest of the evening falling into easy conversation. We share stories and get to know each other even more. More than anything, we're just enjoying our time together, talking and laughing over some absolutely fantastic food. After we pay for dinner, we make it down to the dance floor. But, we only stay for one dance. I make sure to snap a selfie of the two of us for my website. It's not as good as a vlog, but for the rest of the evening, I just want to focus on us. Michael clasps my hand and gently tugs me off the dance floor and towards the front of the restaurant. We walk outside ready to go back to the resort. Both of us are way too tired to even consider staying late tonight.

Michael steps up to the podium just outside the door and asks, "Could you get us a car to bring us back to Ramla Bay Resort?"

"Of course," he replies. Pulling out a radio, he speaks into it and a black sedan pulls up almost immediately making me grin in satisfaction.

"Thank you," we both tell the man as we climb into the back seat and Michael pulls the door closed behind us.

Michael lifts his arm and wraps it around my shoulders, pulling me in close to his side. Glancing up at him, I smile as I settle into him, resting my head on his shoulder. We both sit in comfortable silence, watching the darkened scenery rush by as I think about the last few days and the man sitting beside me. I can't ruin this.

Everything seems so perfect between us. I don't know if I've ever had so much fun with anyone. I quietly huff a laugh. I never would've thought I'd be grateful Kristen didn't come on this trip with me. Let alone, I can't believe I want to spend as much time as I can with Nine-C after how he acted when we first met. A small giggle escapes my lips.

"What's so funny?" he prompts. He looks down at me as the corners of his lips twitch up in amusement even before he knows why I'm laughing.

Glancing up at him, I admit, "You." His eyebrows draw down in confusion making me laugh harder. I catch my breath and elaborate, "I was just thinking about how you seemed like such a different person when I met you on the airplane."

He winces and immediately apologizes again, "I really am sorry about that."

"I know, but I also know why now. I'm just grateful you decided to let me in," I claim. He grins down at me making my heart skip a beat, just as we pull up to the resort.

Taking a deep breath, I tear my gaze away from Michael. I mumble, "Thank you," to the driver and quickly scramble out of the car. Michael pays the driver bringing color to my cheeks, realizing I didn't even think about it. Then he climbs out and steps up next to me. I awkwardly murmur, "Thank you. I wasn't thinking," I admit shaking my head.

He chuckles softly, clearly amused with my frenzied nerves and claims, "I don't mind."

I offer him a sheepish smile in appreciation. Glancing at me, he links his fingers with mine in response, sending goosebumps scattering across my skin. We take our time strolling hand in hand back towards our rooms, just enjoying being near one another. Although I'm exhausted, I'm still hesitant to let the night end. Every moment I'm with him I can't seem to wipe the smile off my face. We have so much fun together that I don't want to let him go. I definitely need to get some rest though. "So, I was thinking," I begin.

"Okay," he prods, dragging out the word.

"So, for tomorrow, since we both seem pretty tired," I add smirking, "I think we need to spend the day relaxing," I emphasize.

He nods his head in agreement, "Yes, please. That sounds perfect. Plus, I believe we have our spa appointment tomorrow," he reminds me.

"That's right," I grin, already looking forward to it.

"We do have a boat reserved for a little while in the morning. Do you still want to do that? Or would you rather just hang out by the pool?" he inquires.

"Well, do you want to do both?" I question. "I think going for a boat ride, relaxing by the pool and going to the spa all sounds pretty relaxing."

He chuckles softly and nods his head in agreement. "You're right. I guess my brother thought about that ahead of time."

"So, I guess I'll see you tomorrow morning for breakfast?" I prompt.

"Absolutely," he confirms, nodding his head. He grins and stares into my eyes, not making a move to walk away.

"Goodnight, Michael," I proclaim with a bright smile on my face.

"Goodnight, Shea," he states softly.

Forcing myself to tear my gaze away from his, I spin around and quickly unlock my door. I push the door open and slip inside, feeling his eyes on me. As the door clicks shut, I fall against it with a heavy sigh and a content smile. Every minute I spend with this man, I find myself falling more and more for him. At this rate, I'm never going to want to leave Malta or maybe it's just Michael I'm not going to want to leave.

Chapter 19

Shea

I take one last sip of orange juice and set my glass back down on the table. "Okay, I'm ready," I announce, grinning at Michael.

"Then, let's go," he prods.

I spot Sam approaching from behind Michael and I wave to him, grinning wide. "Good Morning, Sam," I proclaim, as I stand up from the table.

"Good morning, Miss Shea," he greets me, smiling wide and giving me the same knowing look as he did yesterday. Then he turns to Michael and states, "And a very good morning to you too, Mr. Michael."

"Morning, Sam," Michael replies.

"If you have a few minutes, you can help decorate our Christmas tree in the lobby with one of our candy cane hearts," he informs us.

"Candy cane hearts?" I question, my curiosity piqued.

"Yes," he nods in affirmation. "We have single and entwined candy cane hearts in red and white, white and green, green and red, and even some silver and blue. All we ask you to do is put your names on the heart and hang it together," he explains. "They will be there through Christmas morning," he advises.

"Huh," Michael mumbles. "We just might have to do that."

"Thank you," I say. "Have a good day, Sam."

"Enjoy your day!" he replies.

"Bye, Sam," I wave as we turn and walk away.

We both slip on our sunglasses as we step outside. "Are you wearing your bathing suit under that?" Michael questions. He's wearing simple black board shorts and a white tank top trimmed in black with a colorful design on the front.

I glance down at my own outfit, assessing it. I'm wearing black shorts with a pale yellow tank top and a white wide-knit short sleeve shirt with the knit wide enough to clearly see the yellow underneath. But I am wearing my bathing suit under my clothes. "Yes," I state. "I don't want to have to worry about going back to the room later to change," I admit.

"Good, because it definitely looks like it's going to be a perfect day for the boat and the pool," Michael comments.

He reaches for my hand and entwines our fingers as we walk along the shore, making our way over to the boat rental. The building reminds me of an elaborate shed more than anything. A man about the same height as Michael with short, dark hair, dark skin and soft brown eyes grins as we approach. "May, I help you?" he inquires with a thick accent.

"We have a reservation," Michael announces handing him a piece of paper with our reservation.

Glancing at our paper and then at his own paperwork, he nods in affirmation. "Okay, I have your boat all ready for you. I just need you to sign a few papers and I'll get you two set up right away," he advises.

"Thank you," he replies. The man gives us a quick lesson on the twenty-three foot center console Trophy boat, but Michael knows what he's doing when it comes to boats. Then he makes sure we have our life jackets and other safety equipment on board before we push off the dock.

Taking our time, we make our way out of the cove and staying somewhat close to shore to check out some of the spots we've seen on land from the water. "This is amazing seeing everything from this point of view," I comment.

Speeding up, he turns towards the other end of the island. "Do you want to drive?" Michael questions.

"Really?" I prod, bouncing on my toes in excitement.

He chuckles and nods his head, "Yeah. Come here," he urges, momentarily slowing down the boat.

"Okay," I agree, doing as he says.

He reaches out and helps guide me as he speaks. "Stand right in front of me and I'll help you if you want," he instructs, "but I think you've got this."

Smiling at him, I hold the stainless steering wheel and gently nudge the throttle up, urging the boat to go a little faster. We skim smoothly across the water, barely bouncing, with the wind blowing in our faces and the scent of salt strong in the air. I breathe a sigh of contentment, smiling to myself. "This is perfect," I murmur softly.

"Yes, it is," he agrees, smiling down at me. I feel myself flush, suddenly realizing how close he's standing to me with his hands braced on the console on either side of me helping to maintain his balance.

Clearing my throat, I slow down as I spot a flash of color. "Look!" I say, pointing in excitement. We slow even further before we stop completely, floating up and down on the waves. We drift for a few minutes, looking down over the side of the boat and watching a colorful school of fish near a coral reef sitting close to the surface.

"Wow," Michael murmurs. Stepping back towards the center, he tugs me with him. "I don't want you too close to the edge without me and fall in again," he teases.

167

"Well, at least you wouldn't have to jump off a cliff to save me this time," I joke back.

He chuckles, nodding his head. "True, but it might not be too easy to have to swim after our boat with you in tow." I grimace and he insists, "I'd swim all the way back to the resort with you just to keep you safe."

My heart clenches in my chest, overwhelming me with emotion. Glancing at the time, I sigh and inform him, "Speaking of the resort, I believe we have to head back to return the boat."

"You're right," he concurs. "Do you want to drive back?"

"No, you go ahead," I prod, moving to stand next to him. He spins the boat around with ease and steers it in the direction of the resort, glancing down at me every few minutes. We sit back in comfortable silence, enjoying the ride, the view and the company.

After returning the boat, we make our way over to the pool. Walking around, we're grateful to find two empty lounge chairs and we sit down side by side. Michael's stomach growls making me giggle. "Hungry?" I prod playfully.

He grins and shrugs, offering, "I'll go grab us something to eat. What can I bring you?"

"I'm actually not that hungry," I admit. "Could I just have a strawberry-banana smoothie?" I request.

"Of course," he states and walks away. I slip off my shorts and top, glancing down at my one-piece black bathing suit with straps crisscrossing in the front. Pulling out my sunscreen, I quickly apply it to my face, arms, legs, and front. Then, I attempt to reach my back having no luck.

Michael approaches with a smoothie in each hand, while attempting to balance a plate loaded with a sandwich and fruit in between. I quickly sit up and take it from him, trying to help. "Thank you," I mumble.

"You're welcome," he replies. He sits down on the lounge chair next to me and takes a bite of his sandwich. Glancing at me he offers, "Would you like some?"

"No, thank you, but when you're done, would you mind putting some sunscreen on my back?" I prompt.

"I'm happy to help," he acknowledges. He takes another bite and sets his plate down, scooting to the edge of the lounge chair. He picks up my sunscreen on the table next to me and squeezes some into his hand before reaching for my back. Reflexively, I flinch away at the feel of the cool lotion. "Sorry," he apologizes and continues to rub the lotion into my back and helping me relax.

"I have to say," I mumble as he finishes, "this is really making me look forward to our massages this afternoon."

He chuckles softly and admits, "You and me both."

I sit back on the lounge chair, tilt my head back and close my eyes, enjoying the feel of the warm sun on my skin. Just as I feel myself sinking into sleep, a splash of cold water hits me, and my eyes fly open as I sit up straight with a gasp. "What?" I mumble, mindlessly.

I look towards the water, half expecting to see Michael with a mischievous grin on his face, but I only see a young couple just getting out of the water. The man glances over at me with a look of regret. "I'm sorry," he apologizes.

"It's okay," I respond. I glance over at Michael and ask, "Do you want to go swimming?"

"With you?" he prods, sounding surprised.

"Yes, with me," I laugh, lightheartedly swatting at him.

"Of course," he agrees.

Standing, I walk over to the shallow end like I did the other day and slowly wade into the water. Just as I make it about waist deep, Michael's head pops out of the water right in front of me making me jump. "Hi," he mumbles, grinning.

"You scared me," I inform him. I place my hand lightly on my chest, hoping to calm my racing heartbeat.

Chuckling, he admits, "I can tell." I narrow my eyes at him, making him laugh harder. "I'll carry you on my back," he offers.

"I used to do that when I was a little girl with my dad," I reveal.

Crouching down, he turns and holds his hands out, offering me a ride. "I'll be gentle," he promises.

"Okay," I agree.

Holding tightly to his shoulders, he starts to move a little deeper. "Why don't you put your arms around my neck," he suggests. "It will make it a little easier to swim. Just don't hold on in a death grip like you are now."

Glancing down at my hands, I notice my white knuckles and instantly loosen my grip, moving my hands around his neck. "Oh, sorry." He swims around the pool a couple times with me on his back and I relax against him, my body starting to feel weightless. I suddenly realize one thing. I trust this man with my life and that really scares me. We make it back to the shallow end and I immediately plant my feet on the bottom of the pool.

"Was that so bad?" he prods, playfully.

Shaking my head I respond, "No, not at all."

Lowering himself to his knees, he urges, "Come here. I want to show you something." I hesitate for only a moment before I step over to him knowing he'll keep me safe. "Okay, now come down to my level," he reaches for my hands and carefully pulls me closer. "Now turn around and I want you to lift your feet off the ground." I gasp, my eyes widening with anxiety. "I promise, I will support you the whole time," he murmurs, his voice comforting. "I won't let you go. You will be safe with me," he emphasizes. I nod my head, letting him know I'm trusting him. Then, I turn around and he switches his hands, holding my arms out. "Now lift your feet and push your stomach up as you lay your head back on my shoulder," he directs. My heart picks up its pace as I do as he says. His cheek presses to mine, warming me up and calming my anxiety. He holds my hands out by my fingertips and his voice rumbles throughout my body as he speaks. "Look at you," he croons. "You're doing a back float!"

I gasp in surprise and without thinking, I lift my head to look. His hands quickly slide through the water, gripping me by my waist and helping me to my feet, stopping me before I have the chance to sink even a little bit. "Wow," I mumble, a small smile on my face.

"Nice job," he grins.

I laugh, feeling a burst of excitement rush through me. I spin around, my foot slipping on the bottom. He reaches out, wrapping his arm around my waist and catching me as my heart bounces up into my throat. Looking up at him, I gulp down the lump in my throat and mumble, "Thanks."

He nods his head and places me back on my feet again, taking a step away from me. Clearing his throat, he states, "We should get going if we want to make our spa appointment."

"Okay," I agree, nodding my head and making my way over to the steps. We walk over to our lounge chairs in silence. I quickly dry off and throw my clothes back on over my bathing suit before grabbing the rest of my things. Glancing over at him, I prod, "Ready?"

"For a massage?" he challenges arching his eyebrows. "Definitely," he confirms, answering his own question.

We make our way over to the spa and walk inside. Closing my eyes, I inhale deeply, instantly feeling a change in the atmosphere with the scent of lavender prevalent. Letting my eyes slowly flutter open, I smile at what I see, loving the clean, simple lines of the white and pale blue room, giving it a modern look. We step up to the desk and check in. "Okay, we're ready for you. Let me show you both where you can get changed," she advises. Following her down the hall, she stops in front of two doors, a women's locker room on the left and a men's on the right. She holds out a folded, plush white robe with white cotton slides on top for each of us and we both reach out and grab a set. You can use any locker you like, follow the directions to set the code to lock it, so you're able to unlock it later and then meet me back out here after you're both changed.

"Thank you," we both reply. I smile at Michael and slip inside to change. Wrapped up in the robe, I step into the hall to find Michael already waiting. We follow the same woman further down the hall and she steps into a dimly lit room, holding the door open for both of us. I hesitate for a moment, realizing we're both going into the same room. I guess I didn't think about it when he said couple's massage, but my nerves suddenly become a little chaotic, attempting to wreak havoc on my insides.

"Lia and Alessia will be in to begin your massages in just a few minutes. You can go ahead and get settled underneath the towels," she advises.

Stepping into the room, I gasp in surprise, overwhelmed by both the relaxing and romantic atmosphere. Rose petals are sprinkled all around the room, with two massage tables in the middle of the room wrapped in white towels, with more piled on top. "Thank you," I mumble.

"Yes, thank you," Michael quickly stammers. She steps out of the room and closes the door. "Wow," he mumbles under his breath. I nod my head in agreement and then step up to the table on my right. "I can turn around while you get on the table," he offers. "I promise not to look."

"Thank you," I reply with an appreciative smile. He turns around and I slip off the robe, hanging it on a hook near the table. Then, I slip onto the table and lie on my stomach, pulling the towels carefully over me. "Okay," you can turn around," I advise, closing my eyes as my hair falls down over the end of the table.

I hear him moving around before he announces, "I'm all set. You can open your eyes if you want."

The door opens and two women walk in, but I don't lift my gaze. Someone steps up to my table and crouches down in front of me, "Hi, I'm Alessia. I'll be your masseuse today," she proclaims.

"Hi," I murmur. She soon begins the massage and it takes merely seconds before I'm completely relaxed. I smile to myself, thinking about how much the man next to me has completely taken over my thoughts. He makes me laugh and smile, he causes my heart to race and I want to know everything about him. I don't want our time together to come to an end.

Chapter 20

Shea

After our massages, we both felt completely refreshed and energized. We decided to change and go over to one of the local vineyards on the island and check it out before dinner. We just arrived, but I stopped to use the restroom the moment we got here. Glancing in the mirror, I double-check my reflection. I have my hair loosely pulled away from my face and hanging down my back in waves. I'm wearing a blush pink sundress with spaghetti straps that flares out at my waist and hangs to my knees. It has beautiful ivory, pink and olive green flowers, matched with a thin ivory cardigan sweater over the top. I lean towards the mirror and carefully reapply my lip-gloss. Gently rubbing my lips together, I pull them apart with a soft pop.

I slip my lip-gloss back into my purse and make my way back to the main tasting room. The floors and walls, as well as the bar, tables and chairs are all made of a thick redwood, assisting in giving the whole room the look, feel, and scent of both wood and wine. The walls are decorated with wine themed signs and enlarged images of the vineyard itself as well as smaller ones that have the different stages of the wine process.

I approach Michael, standing and waiting for me at the bar. He smiles the moment he spots me and turns, waiting for me, holding two glasses of white wine. He looks incredibly handsome wearing dark blue jeans and a long-sleeved olive green shirt with a brown button at the top hanging open. He extends his hand, holding one of the glasses out for me and inquires, "Would you like to go for a walk outside or sit in the back?"

"Sure," I agree, both options sounding good. I reach up to take the glass from him, his fingers lightly brushing mine in the exchange. Tingles instantly shoot up my arm from the contact. "Thank you," I mumble.

We make our way outside and behind the main tasting building, strolling past the picnic tables and the gazebo. Michael reaches for my hand and entwines our fingers, holding on tight as we make our way into the perfectly lined rows of grapevines, bringing a smile to my lips. The sounds of the soft jazzy Christmas music playing on the outdoor speakers fades, the further we walk down the row. Taking a sip of wine, I inform him, "I had a lot of fun today."

"Me too," he agrees.

"We've been saying that a lot," I smirk, stating the obvious.

Chuckling softly, he concurs, "It's all about the good company."

"Who would've thought?" I taunt.

He chuckles softly and admits, "I really am grateful for the second chance. The last few days wouldn't have been the same without you."

I'm not quite sure how to respond, but I'm grateful for his words and smile at him, hoping he understands. I feel my face heat and my stomach twists. I take a sip of my wine, attempting to cover up my blush. After a few more minutes, we turn around and quietly make our way back to the elongated, rectangular gazebo, the structure appearing nearly as big as a football field. Climbing the four steps, we find large round tables scattered throughout the structure, along with some open space in the middle. We sit down at a large round table resting in the corner, giving us a spectacular view of the vineyard

175

on three sides with the back of the main tasting room building on the last side. It's incredible!

"I love it here," I murmur. "I never want to leave."

"Yeah," Michael agrees, nodding his head. "It's going to be really hard to go back to real life," he acknowledges.

I take in our surroundings and sigh wistfully. I can't help but feel incredibly relaxed and content sitting here. I think Michael might have something to do with that feeling, but I do love it here. "I think this is my favorite place," I proclaim, a small smile on my face.

"Really?" he prompts, arching his eyebrows in surprise. I don't blame him, we've seen and done so many spectacular things in the last few days.

I nod my head in confirmation and emphasize, "Yes."

"Why?" he questions, curious.

I take a deep breath and exhale slowly, taking a moment to gather my thoughts. "I don't know," I finally concede. "It speaks to me. The smell of the vineyard, the music, the view," I tell him in attempt to explain how I'm feeling.

"...The wine," Michael adds, smirking.

I laugh in response. "Yes, the wine is great," I concur. "It's just really peaceful here," I pause, taking a moment to admire our surroundings. "It kind of sums up everything this trip has been for me," I elaborate.

The corners of his lips curve up and he tilts his head to the side adorably. "What's that?" he prompts.

"Calming. Beautiful. Breathtaking, really," I describe. This is the kind of place where wonderful things happen. "If I ever get married, I want to get married on this very spot," I announce, thinking that might help him understand. This is exactly the kind of place I dreamed of getting married when I was a little girl.

Michael holds his glass up to me, as if toasting me. "Well, be sure to think of me fondly if you do," he urges.

My heart clenches without my consent, while I watch him as he takes a sip of his wine. I laugh in response and shake my head, attempting to rid myself of this feeling I have in the pit of my stomach. I can't imagine being here with anyone besides him, even for my wedding. The thought feels foreign, if not completely absurd. I've only known him for a few days.

A new song begins and Michael pushes his chair back, scraping it against the floor. Standing up, he holds his hand out for me. "Dance with me?" he requests.

"Shouldn't we get back to the hotel?" I inquire, glancing back at the building we just exited from. It will take us some time to travel back to the resort and change for dinner. "We have reservations," I remind him.

He smiles down at me, making my stomach flip-flop once again. "One dance won't hurt," he maintains, his grin giving me goosebumps. I smile up at him and gently place my hand in his. He pulls me up into his arms, keeping hold of my hand. I let my other hand fall to his back, as he wraps his arm around mine and we dance cheek to cheek. We sway back and forth, my heart pounding, at the same time, I feel safe and happy. As the song nears the end, I tip my head back and gaze into his eyes. He looks back at me with a seriousness I can't quite place. The last few notes of the song drift away. I take a step back, out of his arms, feeling the loss, but suddenly needing the distance. He smiles and nods his head before releasing my hand.

"We should go," I repeat.

"Okay," he concurs, nodding his head in agreement.

It takes us both a moment to move, but I finally look away, breaking eye contact. I stride towards the tasting room, and we make our way through the building and back to the front of the vineyard to catch a ride back to our resort. The car ride remains quiet, both of us deep in thought and taking almost no time at all.

We step into the lobby and notice the large faux pine tree Sam told us about earlier, now filled with several candy cane hearts in various holiday colors. "Do you want to put our names on the tree?" Michael questions.

"If you want to," I concur.

"I think we should," he declares and walks closer. He finds one of the employees handing out hearts near the tree. She hands him an entwined heart in red and white for the two of us, along with a dark green marker. He writes his name in one heart and hands me the marker. I lean down and write mine on the other heart connected to his. Then, we approach the tree together and place our ornament right between one reading Candice and Craig and another reading Amy and Lee. We take a step back and look at the tree, the simple gesture making my heart suddenly feel full. "I like it," he comments, giving a firm nod of approval.

"Me too," I concur, feeling my face heat at my admission. Clearing my throat, I turn back to him and ask, "Do you mind if I go upstairs and clean up before we go to dinner? I want to dress-up since it is Christmas Eve," I explain.

"Of course I don't mind," he acknowledges. "I think that's a great idea. I'll do the same. I think I brought something nice I can wear for our Christmas Eve date," he claims, grinning.

We walk upstairs and down the hallway. As we reach our doors, I proclaim, "I'll see you in a little while."

"Absolutely," he confirms. "In an hour?" he questions.

"That's perfect," I concur.

We both retreat to our rooms to get ready for Christmas Eve dinner. I showered just before we left for the vineyard, so I reach for the dress I want to wear tonight and hold it up in front of me. "This is perfect," I mumble to myself. I quickly change, slipping into a silky, brown, wrap dress with white polka dots and sleeves that flare out loosely at my elbow.

Then, I spend my time straightening my hair, wanting to leave it down again tonight. I put on my make-up and glance at myself in the mirror, satisfied with the results. I crouch down and grab a strappy tan sandal with a two-inch wedge heal, slip my foot in and clasp the buckle, before repeating the process with the other shoe.

Walking over to the table, I pick up my phone and check the time. I have a little bit of time before Michael will be back to go to dinner. I hesitate momentarily before unlocking my screen, deciding now seems to be a good time to do another vlog before the night goes any further. I haven't been as up to date while I'm here as I'd thought I'd be. I have no idea what tomorrow will be like, so I should post one today.

Holding my phone up, I tap the red button to start recording. "Merry Christmas Eve, everyone!" I announce. "I hope you're enjoying your day! I have definitely been enjoying mine," I admit cheerfully. "Michael and I have been spending most of the day relaxing today. We went out on a boat this morning and saw Malta from the water, which was spectacular! I definitely recommend doing that if you do decide to visit Malta some day. After that, we spent some time by the pool, swimming and yes, I was swimming too!" I proudly declare, remembering him holding me to help me with my back float.

Forcing my focus back on my phone, I continue. "Then, we went to the spa and got a couple's massage. I

179

don't think I need to tell you how amazing that was," I joke. "And we just came back from drinking some good wine at the most beautiful vineyard. It was so peaceful there. It's definitely a place I'd love to go back to," I admit, thinking about going back with Michael. Taking a deep breath, I continue, "Now, I'm all dressed up for Christmas Eve dinner with Michael at the fancy restaurant here at the resort." I pause, realizing I'm talking more about what Michael and I have been doing together than about Malta itself.

Clearing my throat, I resume, attempting to redirect. "Well, anyway, I just wanted to wish all of you a Merry Christmas! The holiday decorations here are beautiful if you decide to come to Malta for a visit during this time of year. There may not be any snow, but the warm weather doesn't take away from the holidays. The decorations are elaborate and definitely help make it feel like it really is Christmas."

"Well, it looks like it's time for me to meet Michael for dinner, so enjoy your holiday and I'll see you all soon! Ciao for now," I declare and blow a kiss to the camera as always. I tap to end the video and quickly upload it before slipping my phone into my purse.

Before I have a chance to think too much, there's a knock at my door. Taking a deep breath, I smooth down my dress as I make my way over to the door. I pull the door open, finding Michael on the other side, completely taking my breath away. He looks incredibly handsome in a tan blazer with a white button down shirt, the top button hanging open, navy blue dress pants and dark brown dress loafers. Lifting my gaze to his sparkling green eyes, I realize my mouth is hanging slightly open and I snap it shut.

"Wow, Shea, you look stunning," he mumbles, his deep voice rumbling right through me and giving me chills.

"Thank you," I reply. "You look pretty handsome too," I admit grinning. He responds with a huge smile, twisting my stomach into knots. I'm in so much trouble with this man. I think I might need another glass of wine when we get downstairs.

Chapter 21

Michael

I'm glad I dressed up tonight, or I might not be comfortable sitting next to Shea. She looks absolutely gorgeous in an amber dress with small white polka dots. It comes down in a V in the front and wraps around, tying at the side with a thin ribbon. It has a ruffle at the hem and it flares out at her forearms, tying with ribbons there, as well. Then she has a two-inch wedge sandal with amber straps crisscrossing on her feet and ankles. I feel pale in comparison to her, with my white dress shirt, sport coat and navy dress pants, but it's not the clothes. She's not only gorgeous, but everything about her seems to shine everywhere she goes. It's like she radiates beauty in every way. I'm incredibly honored and thrilled to be the man standing by her side.

The evening flies by with a delicious dinner, great conversation, good music, light dancing and delectable wine. It feels like we just stepped out onto the restaurant terrace, but it looks like we're the only ones remaining. I'm dancing slowly, with Shea in my arms, while Sam and a waitress cleanup behind us. The song ends and the music cuts off, signaling it's time to go, but Shea keeps swaying in my arms. "The song is over," I announce.

"No it's not," she claims, still holding me tight.

I sigh, not wanting to let her go, but I think the best thing for both of us is to get some sleep. "Come on, Shea," I attempt to encourage her. "Let's head up. I think we've both had a little too much to drink tonight," I acknowledge.

"It's Christmas Eve," she whines. "We should be celebrating," she proclaims, looking up at me with her sweet smile.

"We are celebrating. Come on, Shea. It's time for bed," I reiterate.

She grins and mumbles, "Bed. I like that."

I step back and look down at her, grinning. "Don't tempt me," I warn her, feeling as if I'm playing with fire.

"Come on, Nine-C," she taunts. "Where's your sense of adventure?" she challenges, playfully, tugging on my blazer as if she's trying to shake some sense into me.

"Okay, Shea," I chuckle. "It's definitely time to go get some sleep. Let's go," I repeat.

I grab her purse for her and hold her hand as we start to walk out of the hotel restaurant, headed towards our rooms. She stumbles and I quickly put my arm out, catching her. She falls right into me and stays tucked into my side. I keep my arm around her to help keep her steady. "We fit together like two puzzle pieces," she claims, making me smile.

She stumbles again and my arm around her tightens, as I hold her steady. "Whoa there, Shea. Let's get you upstairs," I encourage her.

"Sounds good to me," she replies.

Sam approaches the two of us, his eyebrows drawn down in concern. "Is everything okay here?" he probes.

"We're great!" Shea broadcasts, dragging out the word.

"We're fine, Sam. Thanks," I convey.

"Do you need any help?" he offers.

I smile politely and shake my head in response. "No. I'll make sure she gets up to her room safely. Just charge dinner to my room, okay?" I request. "I'll sign for it tomorrow," I inform him, hoping that's acceptable.

He grins and nods in acknowledgement. "Sure thing, Mr. Michael," he agrees. "Good night, Miss Shea."

"Night, night!" she declares loudly.

I feel Sam's eyes on us as I hold on to her and guide her up to our rooms. I'm sure he knows I'll take care of her and get her back to her room safely.

She leans on me and I help her down the hallway on our floor. "Let's get you to your room," I prod.

"Okay," she agrees, a little too easily. "Am I going to get my kiss tonight?" she prompts, causing my heart to skip a beat.

"Not tonight," I sigh, regretful.

She stops in the hallway, narrowing her eyes at me and planting her hands on her hips. "Why not?" she asks, demanding an answer.

"I'd like you to remember it," I answer honestly.

"I'll remember," she insists.

"I don't want to take any chances," I claim.

"I'm not going to black out. I'll remember everything," she maintains. "I never black out. I hardly ever drink!"

She just made my point for me without even realizing it. We had drinks at the vineyard and then we had wine with dinner. Plus, she ate such a light lunch. I grimace, hoping this doesn't hit her too hard in the morning. "You sure drank tonight," I gently remind her.

"So did you," she states, accusingly.

I flinch, not wanting to offend her and nod my head in agreement. "That I did. Which is why we're going to go to sleep and pick this up again in the morning," I proclaim.

She pushes off of me, using my chest as her springboard and attempts to stand up on her own. She wobbles and instantly leans back against me for support. "Whoa," she mumbles.

We take a few more steps and I inquire, "Do you have your key?"

"It's in my purse," she answers.

"Okay," I acknowledge.

"Oh, shoot," she mutters. "I forgot my purse." She spins around and attempts to stagger back towards the elevator. I reach out and gently grasp her by the shoulders, slowly guiding her back before she gets very far.

"No, you didn't," I state, shaking my head. "I have it right here," I inform her. I hold her purse up for her to see.

She gives me a proud smile. "Oh! There it is," she mumbles. "Good job, Mikey," she declares and pats me on the chest.

My eyes widen and I gasp in surprise at the use of my nickname. Leaning against the wall, I question what I already know. "What did you just call me?"

Her eyebrows draw down in confusion. "I dunno," she grumbles.

"You just called me Mikey," I enlighten her, a small smile on my face.

"Oopsies," she mumbles, grinning adorably.

"That's what my brother calls me," I reveal. I like the sound of that on her lips.

"Well whaddaya know," she slurs. "I like your brother. And cheese," she adds, randomly. "Does your brother like cheese?" she asks, tilting her head to the side.

"What?" I chuckle softly and shake my head in amusement. "Oh, Shea, you are so cute tonight," I divulge.

She grins happily up at me, causing my stomach to flip-flop. "Thank you," she acknowledges. "And you're so cute all the time," she discloses, tapping the end of my nose.

My heart skips a beat and I smile in response, but don't acknowledge her comment. We walk the last few steps to her door and I halt her in front of it. "Here you are," I state.

"Here I am!" she announces.

"Do you need me to get your key?" I inquire.

"I can do it myself," she replies, defiantly. I watch as she takes a credit card out of her purse and attempts to use it to open her door. She glares at the door, discouraged. "It's not working," she complains.

I step closer to her and reach for her purse, taking it back from her again. "Here, let me help you," I offer. I peek inside and open her wallet, assuming it's in there, since she pulled out a credit card. I find her room key and pull it out. I slide it into the lock and open the door.

"Yay! You did it," she cheers, praising me.

I smirk in amusement. "I sure did," I agree, nodding my head. "Goodnight, Shea," I tell her, grudgingly.

"What, no hug?" she whines.

I wrap my arms around her and give her a quick hug. I release her, knowing she really needs to get some sleep.

"Come on, Shea. Go to sleep," I encourage.

"Carry me," she states.

I huff a laugh, wondering if I heard her wrong or misunderstood. "What?" I ask.

"Carry me or I'm not going to sleep," she claims.

I heave a sigh and run my hand through my hair, not sure what to do. "Come on now. You're being ridiculous," I mumble in frustration. I'm trying so hard to do the right thing and she's really not making this easy for me.

She puts her hands on her hips and arches her eyebrows in challenge. "I'm allowed one night of ridiculosity," she mumbles, cheekily.

"That's not even a word," I murmur, chuckling softly. I run my hand through my hair again and let out a harsh breath.

"Carry me, Nine-C," she demands, in a singsong voice. "Ooh, I made a rhyme," she proudly declares.

"All right, come on," I relent. It's so hard saying no to her and I'm clearly not getting anywhere arguing with her right now. I crouch down and put one hand behind her back and the other behind her legs, as I effortlessly lift her into my arms. She wraps one arm around my back and falls against my chest.

"Whee!" she squeals.

I prop the door open with my foot and turn my back to the door, pushing it further open for us to step inside. The door slams closed behind us. She begins squirming in my arms, causing me to start struggling. "They make this look so much easier in movies," I grumble. I stride over to her bed and gently lay her down. "Here you go," I state.

I carefully pull my arms out from underneath her, releasing her. I start to stand, but she quickly links her hands around my neck and holds on a little tighter. "Stay the night," she requests, looking into my eyes.

I gulp down the sudden lump in my throat. I grimace as I wiggle out of her hold. "Don't ruin this, Shea," I plead. "We've got a good thing going," I insist.

"I'm not ruining anything," she replies, defensive.

"Shea, I really like you. A lot," I emphasize, trying to get her to understand.

"I like you, like a lot, too," she responds.

"But it's not going to be like this. Not now. Not ever," I reiterate. I want to show her how special she is to me. I want the first time I kiss her to be special and memorable for both of us. It can't be like this, not with her.

Her face falls and she looks up at me from underneath her long lashes, looking like a wounded puppy and breaking my heart. "Am I in the friend zone?" she prompts.

I shake my head and answer insistently, "No, not at all. I just think we've both had too much to drink tonight. Maybe you a little more than me," I concede.

"So?" she prods, her smile contagious. Pulling me close, she whispers, "Guess what? I'm a big girl."

Her warm breath on my neck gives me chills. Taking a deep breath, I exhale slowly, attempting to pull myself together. "Yeah, but not like this, Shea," I plead. "Just please, go to sleep," I repeat.

"I will go to sleep," she begins, wrapping her arms around my neck, "if you give me a goodnight kiss," she pushes, attempting to bribe me.

I grasp her hands and bring them down to her lap. Leaning towards her, I relent. She closes her eyes and tilts her head up towards me, anticipating my kiss. I sigh and move further up, softly kissing the top of her head. She giggles and requests, "Okay, just down a little bit more." I move down, kissing the tip of her nose and she giggles again. "Down," she urges, pointing to her lips.

I kiss her gently on her soft cheek and reiterate, "Go to sleep, Shea." I lean back and look down at her, hoping she understands where I'm coming from. She looks up at me, appearing more resigned than anything. "Goodnight," I whisper.

I watch as she finally rolls onto her side and closes her eyes. I set her purse down on the nightstand, so she'll be able to find it easily when she wakes up. "Goodnight," she mutters, sounding discouraged.

I gently pull off her shoes, wanting her to be comfortable. I reach for the blanket at the bottom of the bed and unfold it, pulling it over her as I go. I walk over to the refrigerator and pull out a bottle of water and set it next to the bed for her, for when she wakes up. I glance at her one more time, appreciating her peaceful beauty, my heart clenching at the sight. Then, I switch off the light next to the bed. Pulling out my phone, I tap the flashlight, before I quietly make my way out of her room. I pull her door shut behind me and chuckle softly. Reaching into my pocket, I grab my key and slip inside my own room, hoping we're both able to get a good night's sleep. I'm really looking forward to spending Christmas with her and hope she feels good in the morning.

Chapter 22

Shea

I wake up, blinking my eyes open with a painful groan. I grimace as I open and close my mouth, hating the pasty feeling and the bad taste. Looking down at the blanket covering me, I roughly push it away. My eyes widen at the sight of my clothes. I'm still wearing the same thing I went to dinner in last night. "Oh, no," I grumble, panic beginning to set in. A wave of embarrassing memories from last night suddenly flashes through my mind. My body heats instantly in embarrassment, even though I'm the only one in the room.

I roll over towards the nightstand and see a full bottle of water sitting right next to the bed. I reach for it, grateful to Michael at the same time, completely mortified. I pry open the top, put the bottle to my lips and tip it back, drinking most of the bottle without taking a breath. My cell phone begins ringing, the shrilling sound making me wince. I set the bottle down and reach for my purse sitting on the nightstand. I quickly dig my phone out and squint my eyes at the screen. Kristen's smiling face lights up my phone. I sigh heavily, my whole body aching as I tap to connect the call.

"Hello?" I answer, groggily.

"Merry Christmas, Shea," Kristen announces cheerfully.

Her cheerful greeting has me wondering if I slept through Christmas. I slowly sit up and put my feet on the floor. "What time is it?" I inquire, my voice still rough with sleep.

"It's midnight," she replies, as if her answer should be obvious. "I wanted to be the first person to wish you a Merry Christmas," she declares.

If it's midnight there, what time is it here? It hurts too much to do the math, so I turn my head, glancing at the hotel clock on the nightstand. "It's six in the morning, Kris," I grumble, realizing I've barely slept.

"Oh, right! Oops," she mumbles. "I'm sorry," she instantly apologizes. "Are you alone?" she questions.

"Of course I'm alone," I retort, dropping back down onto the bed. "I just woke up," I remind her. In fact, I think it's too early to get out of bed.

"Oh, I thought that you and Michael might have...you know..." she stammers, trailing off awkwardly.

"No," I reveal, shaking my head even though she can't see me. "I've known him less than a week," I remind her.

"Well, you never know," she rambles. "Barnaby and I moved fast and look where we are now," she proclaims, proudly. I grimace and roll my eyes, imagining her admiring her two-karat princess cut diamond engagement ring. It's a gorgeous ring, but I believe that man will continue to do everything he can to pull Kristen away from me and I don't want to lose my best friend. I don't understand what his problem is with me. I've been nothing but nice to him. I won't let him tear us apart. Then again, he already started to succeed the day he convinced her not to come with me on this trip we saved for and planned for so long. It makes me wonder if he's really the right man for her, but I can't think about that right now.

I bring my thoughts back to what happened last night and a wave of regret washes over me yet again. "Well, it wasn't for lack of trying on my part," I grumble in response, recalling how much I threw myself at him.

"What do you mean?" she asks, puzzled.

"I had a little too much to drink last night and I asked Michael to stay," I concede, cringing at my own admission.

"And he didn't?" she prompts, sounding surprised.

I shake my head as if she's standing in front of me. "No," I reply and heave a sigh. "He was a perfect gentleman," I emphasize. "I'm still wearing the clothes I wore to dinner last night," I enlighten her, feeling my embarrassment crash into me again.

"Oh. Well," she begins, but trails off, not finishing her train of thought.

"Well?" I probe. "Well what?" I impatiently demand.

"Nothing!" she declares, insistently. "Nothing," she repeats, sounding less convincing. I can practically hear the wheels turning in her head. "Really," she emphasizes, but I don't believe her even a little bit.

"Krissie, what?" I question, almost desperately. I need someone else's opinion on what happened and what I should do to salvage everything with Michael. Plus, I'm having trouble figuring out what he really wants. He said I'm not in the friend zone, but...I don't know. My head feels like a mess of cobwebs, humiliation and regret.

"Well...Nothing, it's nothing," she reiterates. "I'm sure he is totally into you," she emphatically proclaims.

My heart skips a beat, suddenly concerned. Maybe, I've been reading him all wrong. "What would make you think otherwise?" I prod, anxiously.

"Well," she begins, obviously hesitant to disclose her thoughts. I can tell the moment she relents, as she sighs heavily. Speaking softly, she simply states, "He didn't stay with you," and then she emphasizes, "and you asked."

My stomach twists into knots, wondering if she's right, but his reasons could also be the complete opposite of what she's conveying; he's interested and was just trying to do the right thing, so I argue with her anyway. "Because I had too much to drink and he didn't want to ruin things between us," I say, attempting to defend the situation. My mind suddenly jumps to all the worst-case scenarios, causing my heart to lodge itself in my throat. We are on vacation on the other side of the world. We could leave here and he would never have to see me again if he didn't want to. His hesitation could be for a whole range of different things, good and bad. I quickly try to shove the bad reasons out of my head.

"Do you think he has a girlfriend back home and maybe he felt guilty?" she inquires. I cringe, her thoughts going the same place my mind wanted to go to, but I immediately attempted to crush it before it got to me. Just hearing the question out loud fills me up with such anxiety I feel dizzy. I'm grateful I'm already lying down.

There's no way that's true, though, not after how he's been treating me. "What? No!" I insist, hoping I'm right, but what if I'm not? "Why would you think that?" I probe. My heart races as I apprehensively wait for her to answer my question and irrationally hoping her response will ease my worry.

"Shea, look at you," she begins, encouraging me. "You're hot. You're smart. You're caring. You're a real catch, Shea," she emphasizes, complimenting me. "Why wouldn't he jump all over your offer?" she challenges. "I mean, even if it's just to sleep next to you and be close to you, not doing anything else, you know?" she prompts.

My heart drops into my stomach, making me feel sick. She might be right, but I also feel very protective of Michael and I instantly defend him. "You don't know him, Kristen," I snap.

"Neither do you, if you think about it," she reminds me. "I mean, you have only known him a few days," she emphasizes.

She's right, but I feel like I do know him after all the time we've spent together and everything we've shared. I told him things I've never told anyone and he seemed to do the same with me. At least that's what I thought he was doing. "Still," I probe, quietly.

"Shea, you're my best friend. I just want to protect you," she insists and I know it's the truth. I try to do the same thing for her. "I should be there with you and then none of this would even be happening," she states, sounding regretful.

I heave a sigh and reiterate, "But you're not here, Kris. And it has been so amazing here with him," I insist. I pause, trying to think of a good way to explain how I've been feeling since he started to let me in that first morning at breakfast, but it's hard. I've never felt this way before. "It's been like a fairy tale," I finally convey.

"Fairy tales aren't real," she emphasizes. "What are you going to do if you come home and he isn't who or what he says he is?" she prods, asking the hard questions. "It's going to break your heart," she asserts, making me wince.

"You're doing a good job of that yourself, Kristen," I retort, defensively. I can't help but feel both hurt and irritated with her reaction. Michael is a good guy. I know in my heart he is. I can feel it! And he's been acting and talking like he's into me all week. I grimace and concede, well, mostly. It didn't start out that way and then last night...

"I'm just being realistic, Shea," she claims. "When you think about it, you really don't know him. He could have made up everything he told you," she suggests. That's true, but something tells me he wouldn't do something like that. Would he? "We live in a scary world," she mumbles. "If I were you, I'd just come home," she proposes.

My eyes widen in shock and I groan in irritation at her suggestion. "I can't believe you're ruining my trip like this!" I grumble accusingly, even though I know it's my fault this trip has veered in the wrong direction.

"I'm sorry!" she immediately apologizes. "I guess I just feel responsible for everything," she admits. "What if this guy turns out to be some pathological liar that has a wife and baby at home?" she probes, irrationally, but I can't stop wondering if anything she's saying could be true, no matter how ridiculous she might sound. "Say something," she requests, pleading. But I remain silent, thinking about all of the possibilities and unsure what I'm supposed to do. Everything has felt so perfect this week and then I had to go and ruin it. "Please," she begs, sounding as if her guilt from staying home is beginning to weigh her down.

"Merry Christmas, Kristen," I say, quietly. I refuse to comment on her rant when I don't even know what I'm thinking, yet. I disconnect the call, without waiting for her response, knowing she'll be upset, but I can talk to her in a little while, after I figure out my own beliefs. It's honestly too early and I'm too tired to even talk about it anymore.

Dropping my phone down on the bed, I take a deep breath and exhale slowly, feeling defeated. I look around the hotel room, questioning my time this past week with Michael. In my heart, I don't think I really believe anything Kristen is suggesting, but did I ruin everything last night? I don't know how I let that happen. I'm glad he was a gentleman, but I can't believe he even had to ask me to stop. No, that's not true. He practically had to beg me to stop. He warned me, but I refused to listen. I just kept pushing and making him more and more uncomfortable. I'm so incredibly mortified by my behavior. I honestly don't think I can even face him.

I force myself to stand up and get out of bed, the simple movement painful. Trudging over to the mirror I look at myself, grimacing at my reflection. I'm a complete and utter mess. My hair is sticking up all over, my clothes are disheveled, my skin is pale with my makeup smeared all over my face and my eyes looking red and puffy. I shake my head and look away, completely disappointed in myself. Everything was going so well and then I had to go and ruin it. I can't believe I did that. "Merry Christmas, Shea," I grumble, my chest aching painfully.

I sigh heavily and turn towards the closet with my decision made. Opening the door, I pull my empty suitcase out and heave it onto the bed. Unzipping it, I flip it open, glaring at it as if it's to blame. I'll shower and cleanup, but then I think it's time for me to pack. "I guess it's time for me to go home," I mumble to myself, my heart full of regret as a tear slides down my cheek. Closing my eyes, I lift my hand and place it on my aching chest as I take a deep breath, trying to feel better. Opening my eyes, I relent, knowing nothing will help ease the pain at this point. I put myself in this position. Now, I have to work to claw my way back to myself.

Grabbing some clothes to wear to the airport, I turn towards the bathroom. I take another deep breath and attempt to blink back my tears, but my efforts are useless. It just hurts too much. Some day it will feel better knowing I have some incredible memories with an unforgettable man and some beautiful pictures to go along with them. For now, at least I can admit to myself that it's not Malta I'm going to miss, it's the man that I fell in love with while I was here. My chest clenches again and I step into the bathroom as tears silently stream down my cheeks. Closing the door behind me, I step towards the shower, my first step to the end of our fairy tale. I guess my fairy tale doesn't end with the happily ever after.

Chapter 23

Michael

I slip on a pair of faded jeans and a pale green V-neck t-shirt for a touch of Christmas color. I pull my sneakers on and run my fingers through my hair one more time. Glancing at the time for I think the tenth time, I wonder if it's too early to knock on Shea's door. I'm anxious to see her and spend Christmas with her, but I want to make sure she gets enough sleep. Hopefully she's feeling good this morning.

My phone rings and I glance at the screen. At the sight of my mom's sweet smile, I immediately slide my finger across the screen to answer. "Merry Christmas, Mom!" I happily declare. "You're up really early," I observe.

"Merry Christmas, Michael! We miss you! How are you? What are you doing today? Daryl said you had someone to spend Christmas with," she rambles, shooting off her questions without waiting for any kind of response from me.

"Mom, slow down," I request, chuckling and shaking my head in amusement, even though she can't see me.

"Sorry. It's just nice to hear your voice," she claims, "but Daryl's been keeping me updated on your trip and it sounds like you're having a wonderful time," she reiterates.

A sudden wave of regret crashes down on me knowing I'm not there after such a tough year. "Mom, I'm sorry, I'm not there," I begin to apologize.

She immediately interrupts, "Michael, stop. We're doing just fine here," she insists. "Tell me about this girl you're spending Christmas with," she prompts.

I can hear the excitement in her voice and I smile, feeling a rush of emotion as I think about Shea. I reveal, "Her name is Shea and she's pretty amazing, Mom, but I'll tell you all about her when I come home."

"Alright," she reluctantly concedes. "Does this mean I might meet this girl? Darryl said she's really pretty."

"Mom," I warn, laughing.

"Okay, okay," she relents. "I'm already looking forward to hearing more about her," she insists.

"Thanks, Mom," I state knowing it wasn't easy for her to give in so quickly. "I'm actually about to leave to go find her for breakfast," I inform her. "Would you mind wishing everyone a Merry Christmas for me?" I request.

"I'd be happy to," she agrees. "You go ahead."

"Thanks, Mom. I gotta' go," I reiterate.

"I love you, Michael. Merry Christmas!" she proclaims.

"Merry Christmas," I echo, "and I love you too, Mom."

I disconnect the call, not able to wipe the smile off my face. I grab my wallet and my room key, sticking both in my pockets before I walk out the door. My door slams closed behind me and I step up to Shea's door and knock. I rub my hands together in anticipation, while I wait for her to answer. "Merry Christmas, Shea!" I call through the door, so she knows it's me. There's no response, so I knock on the door again and lean a little closer, checking to see if I hear her moving around. "Shea?" I prompt. "Are you up yet?" I ask, knocking again. "Ho! Ho! Ho! It's time for our Christmas breakfast," I announce, playfully. There's still no response, so I knock one last time and tilt my head to the door, listening closely. "Shea?" I prod. "Are you up?"

I sigh and my shoulders sag in defeat as I reluctantly walk away. Then I quickly make my way down to the restaurant in search of Shea. Maybe she already came downstairs and didn't want to wake me, but I can't imagine her missing breakfast. Plus, we've spent every breakfast together since the day we arrived. I can't imagine having breakfast without her. I grin and admit to myself, "And I don't want to." I walk into the restaurant and quickly scan the room, but my hopes begin to sink, not seeing her anywhere.

I spot Sam behind the bar and swiftly make my way over to him. "Hey, Sam," I greet him.

"Merry Christmas, Mr. Michael!" he proclaims. "I didn't see you leaving with Miss Shea this morning," he acknowledges.

"You saw her?" I probe, my eyes wide. I'm anxious to find her.

He nods his head in confirmation, "Yes. She checked out," he enlightens me, his eyes full of regret.

I gasp and my eyes widen in shock, while my heart drops into the pit of my stomach, making me feel sick. "Checked out?" I repeat, feeling like I can barely breathe. "When?" I question, suddenly desperate.

"A couple of minutes ago," he informs me.

"Where is she?" I ask, already searching the room for her again.

"Outside, waiting for the airport shuttle," he reveals.

I turn towards the front door and then quickly spin back towards him, feeling like I need something big for her right now. I can't let her leave. I don't want to let her go. "Oh, Sam. Do you still have my surprise ready for tonight?" I inquire.

He nods in confirmation and answers, "Yes, Sir, of course."

"Can you get it set up now?" I request.

"Now?" he reiterates.

I nod firmly in verification. "Yes. Right now," I emphasize.

He grins and nods his head in acknowledgement. "Yes, Sir. Sure, Mr. Michael," he happily confirms, saluting me for emphasis.

"Great! Thanks," I mumble. I spin on my heel and sprint across the room and out the front door, intent on stopping her.

I spot her the moment I step outside, a small sense of relief coming over me at the sight of her. She stands on the other side of the fountain, holding the handle of her black suitcase and another bag over her shoulder. She's wearing faded blue jeans and a short sleeved, pale pink, ribbed shirt. Her silky brown hair is hanging loose down her back. She looks absolutely beautiful in the sunlight, nearly taking my breath away. My stomach twists with nerves. I have to convince her to stay. I can't lose her. I jog around the fountain as I call out to her, "Shea! Shea!"

She turns around slowly, her eyes widening in surprise. "Michael! What are you doing?" she questions as I come to a stop in front of her.

"Me?" I ask gesturing to myself. "What are you doing?" I emphasize and arch my eyebrows in challenge.

My heart clenches, as I watch her face fall with regret. "I ruined everything," she grumbles. She lifts her gaze to mine, her eyes filled with so much sadness it breaks my heart. "I'm going home," she announces.

I shake my head in refusal. I'm not letting her go. "No, you can't," I declare. I know we were meant to be. I feel it even more at the possibility of losing her.

"I made a complete fool out of myself last night," she mumbles, sounding as if her own heart is breaking.

"No, you didn't," I claim, shaking my head in denial.

She nods her head firmly and reiterates, "I did! I never drink that much. Ever," she stresses. "I can't believe I did that," she mumbles, shaking her head in disbelief, her disappointment in herself obvious.

"Shea, relax," I plead. "I drank, too," I remind her, hoping it will help ease her mind. "It's fine," I insist.

"Not as much as I did," she mutters, scrunching her nose up with distaste.

"So?" I prompt, shrugging my shoulders. "If I did, then we would both regret it." I pause, attempting to think of the right thing to say or more accurately, the right way to say what I'm thinking. "Shea, we all make mistakes," I emphasize, trying to let her know we can get past this.

"Yeah," she concedes, grimacing. "But, I feel like I've made so many on this trip," she claims, her eyes full of remorse.

I wince, hoping she's not talking about me. "So have I," I state, remembering how terrible I was to her at first. "I was such a jerk to you when we met, remember?" I prompt, arching my eyebrow in challenge.

She giggles in response, easing some of the tension out of my shoulders. "That seems like a lifetime ago," she admits.

The corners of my mouth curve up with hope at her reaction. "Yeah, and you forgave me," I emphasize. "You gave me another chance," I repeat.

She grimaces and reiterates, "Yeah, but I was such an idiot last night."

My chest tightens and I shake my head, refusing to let her walk away from us because of this. "Shea, I jumped off a cliff for you," I remind her of the extremes I'll go to for her. "Don't leave. Please," I beg, desperate.

She looks up at me, appearing at a loss for words. She opens her mouth and snaps it closed again, just as the shuttle for the airport pulls up. "Going to the airport?" the man questions, calling out the window of the van.

She lifts her gaze to mine again with her mouth open, ready to speak. The look on her face tells me she's still hesitant to stay causing my heart to feel as if it stops completely. "Michael, I," she begins, her tone apologetic.

I instantly interrupt her, not letting her get the words out that could take her away from me. If she's going to walk away from us she needs to do it knowing everything. My heart kick-starts, pounding erratically and my stomach twists into knots in both fear and anticipation, but for her I'll always take the leap. "Shea, I'm falling in love with you," I blurt out. The moment the words leave my lips, I know the depth of their truth. I've never felt this way before about anyone. She makes me happier than I've ever been and she makes me want to be a better man. I want to be that man for her and with her. I just hope she feels the same way.

She gasps and her eyes widen in shock. "What?" she questions. She shakes her head softly as if she may not have heard me correctly.

I take a step closer to her and repeat myself with more confidence. "You can't leave because I'm falling in love with you," I declare, with a smile on my face and my heart full.

She looks down at the ground and I hold my breath in anticipation of her response. "I..." she mumbles and trails off, looking around as she gathers her thoughts. My whole body feels tight, hoping I didn't just make everything worse.

My heart feels like it's about to burst. I don't think I can wait another second. I have to know what she's thinking. "Will you please say something?" I cry out, pleading.

She looks up at me from underneath her long lashes with a change in her eyes. The corners of her mouth tug upwards, causing my heart to skip a beat and fill with hope. "Will you help me with my bag?" she requests. "It's kind of heavy," she adds. A bright smile consumes her face and I breathe a sigh of relief.

I nod in confirmation, as my whole face lights up with my smile and I feel my whole body exhaling in relief. I step towards her and reach for her bag, taking it from her as I nod in agreement. "Yeah," I murmur. She didn't respond to my confession, but right now, I don't need her to. I just need her here with me so we have a chance.

She turns towards the car waiting for her and smiles in appreciation as she waves the airport shuttle driver on. "I'm sorry, but I don't need a ride anymore. Thank you," she proclaims. He nods his head in acknowledgement and drives away.

I turn and stride back to the hotel as quickly as possible with her bags. I don't want to take the chance that she might change her mind again if I wait even one extra moment. Sam grins at me as I walk inside with her suitcase and extra bag in my hands. "Would you be able to keep her bags behind the front desk for her for a little while?" I inquire.

He nods in agreement, "Of course. Where's Miss Shea?"

"She's coming," I proudly proclaim. I grin broadly and nod towards the front door. I turn towards the desk clerk as I set her things down. "Could you direct her to the terrace when she walks in?" I request.

"Absolutely," he agrees, nodding his head.

"Thank you," I assert. Then, I jog towards the terrace, anxious to get out there before she walks inside.

Chapter 24

Shea

I stand still for a moment, watching the airport van pull out of the resort drive and disappear down the street, with a smile on my face. I'm a little bit in shock by what just happened. My heart pounds so hard inside my chest that it feels as if it might burst or break right through my ribcage. Is this real? Did Michael really just say he's falling in love with me? Even after I acted so foolishly last night? I shake my head in disbelief and spin around with excitement, retreating back towards the resort. I need to go talk to him. I need to know if what he said is true, but just knowing there's definitely something between us and it's not just me, seems to have given me a bounce in my step that definitely wasn't there before. I feel like I'm the luckiest woman in the world!

I'm surprised to find Michael didn't wait for me; he already disappeared inside the hotel with my bags. I quickly pick up my pace, jogging to catch up with him. I pull the door open and step into the lobby. I halt, looking around for Michael, but I don't see him anywhere. "Where did he go?" I mumble to myself, my eyebrows drawn down in confusion. Why would he say all of that to me and then completely disappear with my bags? I giggle to myself, finding it somewhat amusing. Suddenly, I notice my suitcase and bag sitting right next to the front desk without Michael, puzzling me even further. I quickly scan the lobby and glance into the restaurant, looking for him one more time, before I finally call out for him, not sure what else to do. "Michael? Where did you go?"

The hotel clerk who checked me in the day I arrived waves his arms wildly, trying to get my attention. "Excuse me!" he calls from across the lobby. I turn and start striding towards him. He offers me a wide grin and happily enlightens me, "If you're looking for Mr. Michael, he's out on the restaurant terrace."

Perplexed, but grateful for the information, I smile at him in appreciation. "Thank you," I respond and wave.

"You're welcome," he replies. Then, he brings his focus back to the guests standing in front of him at the desk.

I quickly make my way over to the French doors at the back of the restaurant and push the door open, stepping outside onto the terrace and closing the door behind me. The guitarist rounds the corner and starts strumming his guitar the moment I close the doors, bringing a smile to my face. I look over at him standing on the edge of the terrace and smile, wondering what he's doing playing out here when there's no one else around.

Out of the corner of my eye, I see Michael stepping forward, and I immediately spin towards him, giving him my full attention, my heart skipping a beat. I grin even wider as I stare at Michael with a look on his face I don't know if I've ever seen before. It's at that exact moment that I suddenly recognize, the guitarist is playing our song, the realization making me gasp. It's the same song he had written on the spot during my first dinner with Michael. He's playing it for us...for me. My heart pounds so hard inside my chest, increasing the rush of blood in my ears causing almost everything besides Michael to fade into the background. "What's going on? What is all this?" I prompt, my stomach twisting with anticipation.

"Merry Christmas, Shea," Michael declares, grinning down at me. He steps closer to me and holds his hand out, reaching out for mine. I joyfully relent and he clasps our hands together. Glancing down at our joined hands, he gives mine a squeeze, holding it tightly between us, as if he never wants to let it go...let me go.

I lift my gaze and look up into his sparkling green eyes, feeling as if I'm exactly where I'm meant to be. But I need to be sure. I have to know exactly how he feels. "Did you mean what you said out front?" I prompt, desperate for it to be true. Butterflies instantly take flight in my stomach, the moment I have the courage to ask him the question. Taking a deep breath, I exhale slowly; attempting to calm my nerves, while I anxiously wait for his response, hoping everything about this moment, about us, is real.

He gives me a crooked smile and nods his head in affirmation. "I did," he confirms, confidently, my breath catching in my throat. "I do," he promptly corrects himself, not taking his eyes off me. Goose bumps instantly dance across my skin, and my chest feels tight as I notice the sincerity in his sparkling green eyes making it hard to breathe. "I know it hasn't even been a week, but I feel like I have known you my entire life," he claims vehemently.

"I feel the same way, Michael," I finally blurt out my confession. "And I'm falling in love with you, too," I declare, needing him to know how I feel. His face lights up even more at my admission, causing my heart to beat a little faster. I shrug my shoulders, feeling my face heat as I concede, "I guess I just felt silly saying it out loud when it all happened so fast. I didn't think you could possibly feel the same way about me."

He chuckles, smirking at my comment and shakes his head in disbelief. He taunts, "Well, one of us had to say it, right?"

I can't help but laugh in response as I feel myself blush a deeper shade of red. "True," I murmur, grateful he's brave enough to take the leap for both of us.

"Look," he begins, taking a steadying breath, "I don't know where this is going to go when we get home and we jump back into the reality of every day life, but I definitely want to see this through and find out," he emphasizes. My heart clenches with happiness. This doesn't have to end when we leave Malta. He wants to be with me too. Pausing, he quirks his eyebrow and tilts his head to the side, joking, "I mean, I've never started a relationship by having a honeymoon first, but..." The corners of his mouth twitch up in amusement as he trails off.

I laugh at his comment. I had always thought of this as my dream vacation. Then again, we did kind of start this between us with someone else's honeymoon. Most of the activities we've done have been because of his brother and his ex. Let alone, we took their seats on the plane. I laugh at the reality. It has been a dream vacation. It's just not exactly what I had been expecting, but it's definitely a dream vacation all the same and ironically, more than I could've ever dreamed. I giggle softly and shrug my shoulders. "Neither have I," I gladly concur.

He sighs happily as he looks down at me in awe. "You're funny. You're smart," he begins complimenting me.

"And pretty," I tease.

He chuckles softly and nods his head in agreement. "You're definitely pretty," he reiterates, emphasizing the point and making me laugh. "And we fit together, like two puzzle pieces," he proclaims with awe.

My face falls, remembering uttering those same words last night. "I said that when I was..." I mumble, shaking my head.

"Yeah and I'm saying it now," he states firmly, interrupting me.

I smile at him, comforted by his conviction. "It's a good line," I claim, shrugging my shoulders like it's no big deal.

"Yeah, I agree," he concurs, grinning and nodding his head. "I told you that you should be a writer," he asserts.

I nod in appreciation, but I glance at him, needing to explain my reasoning behind my words. "It's not just a line, though, Michael. I mean it," I argue, glancing up at him from underneath my eyelashes. "I've been thinking about it all week. When I'm with you, we have so much fun together. We talk, we laugh, I'm able to be myself and I'm just happy," I explain, shrugging my shoulders. "No matter what we're doing, all I have to do is look over at you and I'm glad that you're the one by my side. It feels like everything kind of falls into place when we're together, like two puzzle pieces. I guess I just needed some liquid courage to say it out loud," I admit, sheepishly.

"Yeah," he mumbles in understanding, giving me a look that leaves us both open and vulnerable and leaving me no doubt about my feelings for him. Clearing his throat, he turns the conversation in another direction. "Remember when you said that we were supposed to be here?" he prods, reminding me what I said at our very first breakfast after we arrived, the one before he jumped. I do, but I can't believe he remembers that. "Well, I think you're the reason I'm supposed to be here, Shea," he declares, looking into my eyes. "I think I was supposed to come on this trip just to meet you," he reiterates. My heart skips a beat in response, before it begins to race nearly out of control, making it hard for me to catch my breath.

I open my mouth to respond, when white flakes begin to fall between us making me gasp in surprise. My eyebrows draw down in confusion and I take a step back looking up, my hand slipping away from his as I put one hand up to shield my eyes from the sun and what appears to be snow falling around us. "What in the world?" I question, puzzled. A giggle escapes through my lips, amused with the supposed change in weather.

He chuckles softly at my reaction and smiles down at me with love and adoration. "Well, I thought I'd bring you a little bit of home for Christmas," he announces cheerfully. "Merry Christmas, Shea."

I narrow my eyes, squinting up above the snow and finally notice Sam on a balcony to my left and the hostess from the restaurant, standing with one of the waitresses from the restaurant on another balcony to my right, all of them carefully shaking snow down onto our heads. I giggle, completely delighted and a little overwhelmed with how amazing this is; how incredible I think Michael really is for doing this for me. Holding out my hands, I tilt my face up towards the sky enjoying the tropical snowfall. I spin around slowly and giddily murmur, "I love this so much!" Halting, I drop my hands to my sides, and turn my head, looking at Michael with a huge smile on my face as I shake my head in wonder. I can't believe he did all this for me. "Thank you," I declare, my heart feeling as if it's overflowing for the man standing in front of me.

He returns my smile and I step towards him, standing toe to toe. He reaches out and pulls me close, wrapping his arms around my back. Then, he tilts his head down towards me, while I tip mine up to look at him, attempting to portray how I feel. He glances into my eyes, before his gaze drifts down to my lips and then he brings his gaze back to my eyes, letting me know his intention. I link my fingers around the back of his neck and push up on my toes, meeting him halfway as he slowly closes the distance between us. A light gasp escapes my lips, just before his soft lips finally press against mine in our first kiss, heating me from the inside out. He gently moves his mouth in perfect rhythm with mine as I completely lose my heart to this man, while the snow slowly falls all around us. Everything about this moment feels like a dream, or maybe this is our fairy tale.

I fall back on my heels, breaking our kiss. We smile at one another as his forehead drops to mine and we both catch our breath. "That was definitely worth the wait," he rasps. "You," he emphasizes, "were worth the wait."

"So were you, Michael," I insist, overwhelmed with emotion. Gulping down the lump in my throat, I whisper, "Merry Christmas." He grins and then lifting his forehead from mine, he again closes the distance between us. He presses his lips to mine in another sweet kiss, as we begin dancing in each other's arms, with the guitarist still playing our song.

Epilogue

Two years later...

Shea

I can't believe it's been two years since we were here in Malta. It's been two years since I met Michael and now we're back at the same vineyard I had told him I wanted to get married at some day. Little did I know, he would be the one standing alongside me on the altar, even if that's what I had hoped would happen some day. The way I talk and laugh with him is something I've never experienced, not even with Kristen. I believe we were truly meant for each other and he's definitely the man of my dreams and my fairy tale. I wouldn't be standing here in a beautiful white dress, designed just for me, if I didn't believe that with all of my heart. I'm so excited to walk down that aisle and marry Michael, my best friend and the love of my life. I can't wait to see him in his tuxedo standing at the end of the aisle waiting for me.

I glance down taking one last look at myself in the mirror. My dress is a beautiful white satin form-fitting, strapless dress underneath, then it has a beautiful lace overlay hemmed with the same satin along all the edges, with two-inch thick straps over my shoulders, coming down in a sweetheart neckline. There's a one-inch thick satin ribbon tied around my waist and connected with a ruby, crystal and pearl broach. The back connects with small satin buttons starting at the base of my neck, with a round opening, leaving part of my back bare, then the small satin buttons continue trailing down from the middle of my back to the lower part of my waist. I have my hair pulled up loosely at the crown of my head, with loose curls pinned down in an elegant bun, enhanced with baby's breath and a small red rose. My earrings match the broach, having the red and white symbol of Malta, made with, rubies, crystals and pearls. I love that I'm wearing a symbol of Malta, where our life together began. Plus, Chris, a very close friend of our family and an incredible designer made every piece of my jewelry for me, making all of it even more special to me.

"Are you ready?" Kristen questions as she steps back into the room. She's not only my best friend, but also my maid of honor and the only one I have standing up for me today. I'm so happy to have her here by my side. She looks beautiful in a sleeveless, A-line red dress with a sheer overlay near her neckline and then it cinches at the waist with a silver ribbon tied at the side. The bottom is enhanced with embroidered flowers and falls to just above her knees. Her silver two-inch high-heeled sandals match the ribbon at her waist perfectly. She has her light blonde hair pulled up into an elegant bun, similar to mine without the enhancements and a few wisps of her hair falling to the side in the front.

I grin, my excitement and pure happiness, palpable. "I'm more than ready," I confidently proclaim.

She smiles and links her arm through mine. "Well, then let's go," she announces. We make our way outside arm in arm and stroll around to the back of the vineyard where the ceremony will begin to prepare for our entrance. We reach the back and stand in front of the rows and rows of grapes, while in front of us the grass is lined with rows of white folding chairs, separated down the middle with a white runner to create an aisle. All the chairs along the aisle as well as several in between are wrapped with white tulle and tied with a bow at the back of the chair. Every single seat already filled with our friends and family who made the trip to Malta to join us for our wedding.

The elongated rectangular gazebo overlooking the vineyard has been transformed into our altar. The wide opening and the rails coming down are wrapped with white tulle and a leafy green garland with small red flowers. The same decoration loops at the top as it swings across the opening, with a white poinsettia connecting the garland and tulle in the middle. At the base of the rails on both sides, a large white poinsettia tops off the ends, bringing it all together.

The priest stands at the top of the altar with a smile on his face, wearing elegant ivory robes with the red flower of Malta embroidered in several different places, as well as a thick gold ribbon emblazoned along the hems. He's a tall man with short dark hair, a neatly trimmed beard and mustache, soft brown eyes and a kind smile.

Michael stands at the altar with his brother Daryl standing proudly by his side as his best man. They both look incredibly handsome in black tuxedos, crisp white shirts and a pink tie. Michael's tux is just a touch dressier than his brother's to help him stand out, but in my eyes, he already stands out all on his own. My heart skips a beat at the sight of him and then restarts, taking off at a gallop. I'm so ready to marry that man.

The music starts up, giving us our queue. "I'm so happy you're here with me this time, Kristen," I tell her.

"Me too, Shea, but I wouldn't have missed this for the world. I'm never letting someone get between me and my best friend ever again," she claims. I smile at her and she grins, giving my hand a squeeze of encouragement before she starts down the aisle.

My dad steps up to stand beside me with a proud grin on his face. Leaning down towards my ear, he whispers, "How are you doing, Kiddo?"

His question squeezes my heart, warming me from the inside out. Taking a deep breath, I lift my gaze and look him in the eyes, hoping he can see the truth in them when I respond. "I'm absolutely wonderful, Dad," I declare.

He smiles, his eyes sparkling with happiness at my response. He has his gray hair perfectly styled and looks incredibly handsome in his black suit, pale blue shirt and silver tie. He holds his arm out for me and I link my arm through his. He pats my hand gently, inside the crook of his arm, as I watch his Adam's apple bob up and down. "I love you, Sweetheart," he rasps, the emotion in his voice apparent.

I know all I can do is respond. "I love you too, Dad," I tell him, struggling to fight off my own emotions.

We both take a deep breath and exhale slowly as the music changes for my entrance. This is a moment I've waited for my entire life and I don't want to ever forget it. I take a step forward, walking side by side with my dad down the aisle. After the first few steps, my gaze lands on Michael. He looks at me smiling so brightly, my knees go weak and I grasp my dad's arm a little tighter for support. He gazes at me with so much love, as if I'm the only one he sees. We reach the altar and my dad gives me a hug and a kiss on my forehead like he did when I was a little girl. Taking my hand, he gives it to Michael, shaking his hand in the process. "Take good care of my girl," he prompts.

"I promise," Michael declares. My dad gives him a firm nod of approval and steps away, taking his seat in the front row next to my mom. Michael takes me by the hand, sending tingles up my arm, as we step closer to the priest, smiling happily at one another.

Most of the short ceremony goes by in a blur. I stare at Michael, not able to wipe the smile off my face. I do what I need to do and say what I need to say, but my focus is completely on Michael. "Do you, Shea Andrews, take this man to be your lawfully wedded husband, to have and to hold, in sickness and in health, as long as you both shall live?" the priest prompts.

I grin at Michael, feeling as if my happiness is about to burst out of me. Without hesitation, I declare, "I do."

The minister turns to Michael and repeats the sentiment, "And do you, Michael Foster, take this woman to be your lawfully wedded wife, to have and to hold in sickness and in health, as long as you both shall live?" he prods.

Michael smiles proudly at me, his green eyes shining brightly with emotion as he proclaims, "I do."

The minister looks back and forth between the two of us as he finishes the ceremony. "By the power vested in me, through the government of Malta, I now pronounce you husband and wife," he announces. "You may kiss your bride," he states.

Michael instantly closes the distance between us as if he can't wait another moment. He cradles my face in his hands, as I grasp onto his wrists for support. He grins and presses his soft lips to mine, his kiss still sending chills down my spine and making my stomach flip-flop. We break the kiss and gaze into each other's eyes for a moment, sharing our joy, happiness and hopes of the future with a simple look that holds so much power between us.

"Looks like you're stuck with me forever, Nine-C," I tease, smiling broadly.

He chuckles softly, grinning wide. "I think I'm okay with that," he proclaims. It feels as if my heart is soaring, as he gives me another chaste kiss. Then, he reaches his hand out for mine and I happily slip my hand in his, entwining our hands together, before we turn to our small group of friends and family for the first time as husband and wife. The moment feels surreal.

The minister looks up at the group of people surrounding us and holds his hands out wide as he broadcasts, "I now present to you Mr. and Mrs. Michael Foster!"

Everyone bursts into loud cheers and applause as we walk back down the grassy aisle, hand in hand and ready to start our forever the same place it all began.

Kristen

I'm so happy for Shea. I can't believe I was so wrong about Michael, but I'm incredibly happy to be proven wrong this time. My doubts probably had something to do with how poorly everything was going with Barnaby and how guilty I felt for not going on the trip with Shea, but I guess in the end it was good I didn't come. I pinch my lips together and immediately try to push Barnaby out of my thoughts. I'm so happy I didn't marry that man. It would've been a terrible mistake.

I watch Shea and Michael for a moment as the two of them retreat down the aisle. They're so obviously in love, their happiness practically radiates off of them in waves. Then, I look across at the best man as we step towards one another, ready to walk back down the aisle. Shea was right. He's an incredibly good-looking man, with a smile that makes my heart skip a beat. He holds his arm out for me and I link my hand through, resting my hand around the bend in his elbow. The simple contact shoots tingles throughout my body and I quickly take a breath to calm my now racing heart.

He tips his head towards me as we stroll leisurely down the aisle. "You know," he begins, "I'm the reason they're together," he claims, proudly.

"Are you?" I prompt, arching my eyebrow in challenge. "I actually left Shea at the airport right before our trip," I reveal.

"Yeah?" he questions and I nod my head in confirmation. "Well, I left Mikey at the airport and gave Shea my seat," he reveals.

"Ooh. Yeah, that's good," I concur, connecting the story Shea had shared with me before with the man walking beside me.

"Yeah, I know," he replies, with an adorable smirk on his face. "They better name their first kid after me," he says, I think only half joking. Then we both burst out laughing. He glances at me, his eyes slightly narrowed, as if trying to put together a puzzle. "You're the friend that cancelled the trip because of your fiancé, right?" he inquires.

I wince in response. "Yeah, don't remind me," I grumble, rolling my eyes in frustration. Just thinking about it still drives me crazy.

Glancing in my direction before returning his focus to the aisle in front of us, he arches his eyebrows in question and probes, "How's that working out for you?"

I hold up my left hand, wiggle my bare fingers at him and smile. "It's not," I announce, playfully, carefully assessing his reaction.

His eyes widen in surprise. "Really?" he prompts, pursing his lips in curiosity. I nod my head in response and I notice a small flicker in his eyes, causing my breath to catch momentarily in my throat. "You know," he begins,

"I hear that Malta is a great place to fall in love," he proclaims with a sparkle in his eyes.

My stomach flip-flops at his comment and I feel my cheeks turn pink. "Is that so?" I question, coyly. The corners of my mouth tug upwards, while my heart fills with hope, as I walk side by side with Daryl following behind Shea and Michael to celebrate their happy ending. Maybe fairy tales are real.

The End

Acknowledgments

This is hard to even begin to thank everyone who has been involved with this book. First, I'd like to thank Olivia and Jonathan Liveng who were not only the executive producers of the film, but the story itself was also inspired by how the two met, although this is not their story! Olivia and Jonathan are often found traveling to spectacular places all around the world and sharing their travels with all of us! Without you both, this movie or book would have never come to be. I would also like to thank Amy Minter who was our US producer and Katryna Samut-Tagliaferro who was our Maltese producer. Both of these women are incredible and we couldn't have done it without either of you! Thank you to Benjamin Bryant for being the supervising producer on the film and Tommy Zamberlan for being the associate producer. I truly enjoyed working with you both on set!

My next thank you is for director and writer, Candy Cain. She is an enthusiastic, motivated and strong woman who I'm grateful to be able to call my friend. This film threw her some unique challenges, yet she always found a way to power through and get things done in the end. Your drive and your determination set you apart from many and it's inspiring. I'm thrilled to be a part of it all along with you. I'm already looking forward to our next adventure.

Thank you to the very talented Ashley Brinkman and Cody Calafiore who brought Shea and Michael to life both on-screen and on the pages. I truly enjoy working with both of you! Clayton Snyder, Abigail Hawk and Lawrence Oliver Cherry, thank you for helping make every day on set so much fun with your smiles, and stories between all your hard work. As for the rest of the cast and the incredible crew, thank you for everything you do and all of your support! I'm thankful that you were all part of our team!

Thank you to Benjamin Bryant again for the fabulous picture I used for the cover and Heartly Creations for the beautiful book cover design.

Thank you to Kelley and Nancy as well as all of my Beta readers for all of your support. I love to write for all of you and all the other people who love reading my books. Without fans, I don't know where I would be right now and I appreciate every single one of you!

Most of all I need my family and friends to know how much I appreciate them! I'm incredibly grateful for your endless support and encouragement in all that I do! Thank you and I love each and every one of you! Hopefully I will be able to spend more time relaxing and like in this book, traveling with you!

I hope everyone is able to take some time to relax while reading and then watching, "The Maltese Holiday," and relish every minute of it! Plus, since this book is being released for Christmas in July, no matter the time of year, Merry Christmas!

Connect with the Author

For more family contemporary romance, read more by Nicole Mullaney and Ethan Dulane. Connect with Nicole here:

Follow Me on Instagram
@nicolemullaney

Author Facebook Page
www.facebook.com/Nicole-Mullaney-Author-103006415283835/

BookBub
@NicoleMullaneyAuthor

For adult contemporary romance, read books by Nikki A Lamers. Connect with Nikki here:

Official Author Website
www.nikkialamersauthor.com

Author Facebook Page
www.facebook.com/pg/NikkiALamersAuthor

Follow Me on Instagram & BookBub
@NikkialamersAuthor

Author Goodreads Page
www.goodreads.com/author/show/8451774.Nikki_A_Lamers

Amazon Author Page
https://www.amazon.com/Nikki-A.-Lamers/e/B00NU1VU8M

For more information on Gemelli Films, find them here:

Official Website for Gemelli Films
http://Gemellifilm.com/

Gemelli Films Facebook Page
https://m.facebook.com/GemelliFilms/

Follow them on Instagram
@Gemellifilms

About the Author

Nicole Mullaney has always had a passion for reading and writing, especially romance. She grew up in Wisconsin with her sister and mom and dad. She always loved reading romance books and watching romance movies with her dad, something they both enjoyed. She now lives on Long Island in New York with her husband and two kids. She spends her free time reading or hanging out with friends and family.

She met Candy Cain through her daughter Allison's acting career. A few years later, at the end of 2018, she began collaborating with her on these film/book projects; Ivy & Mistletoe their first project together in this capacity. She enjoys being able to watch the stories come to life in different ways and be a part of it from the beginning.

www.ingramcontent.com/pod-product-compliance
Lightning Source LLC
Chambersburg PA
CBHW051529280626
47161CB00022B/2918